People, Places, Possibilities

People, Places, Possibilities

Edited & Compiled by
Dr. Geetanjali Patil Pawar
Anushree Gupta
Vaishnavi Singh Rajput
Oindrila Ghatak

Paperback Edition

First published in India in 2023 by

Inkfeathers Publishing
Vivek Vihar, New Delhi 110095
www.inkfeathers.com

ISBN 978-93-90882-97-7

Edited & Compiled by

Oindrila Ghatak

Anushree Gupta

Vaishnavi Singh Rajput

Dr. Geetanjali Patil Pawar

Inkfeathers Publishing

www.inkfeathers.com

Disclaimer

The anthology "People, Places, Possibilities" is a collection of 20 short stories and 28 poems written by 36 authors who belong to different parts of the world.

Unless otherwise indicated, all the names, characters, objects, businesses, places, events, incidents—whether physical/non-physical, real/unreal, tangible/ intangible in whatsoever description used in this book are either the product of the author's imagination or used in a fictitious manner. Any resemblance to actual persons, objects, entities, living or dead, or actual events is purely coincidental.

The contents published in this book are solely owned by their respective authors and are in no way intended to hurt anyone's religious, political, spiritual, brand, personal or fanatic beliefs and/or faith, whatsoever. In case, any sort of plagiarism is detected in the contents within this anthology or in case of any complaints, grievances, or objections, neither the anthology editor nor the publisher is to be held responsible.

Featuring the writings of

Nilkesh Sonawane, Aanika Gajendragad, Vaishnavi Tawade, Kali Sitholey Rawat, Sandhita Agarwal, Aditya Jhingan, Reggie Menacherry, Claire Casapao, Mridini Borate, Rakshana Ramamurthi, Sanskriti Jain, Shaymi Shah, Tejase Rathod, Ammarah Safaa, Mihai Cojocaru, Halo Golwin, Neeraja Krishnaswami, Arshpreet Kaur, Riya Varshney, Anushka Verma, Arpita Mukherjee, Tejaswini Mittal, Mukunda Maheshwari, Anvi Gupta, Dr Varsha Bangarshettar, Chitra Lele, Komal Joshi, Madhumathi J Dharwar, Ranjini Sasidharan, Namrata Agarwal, Sunitha Kolar, Chitra Balsubramaniam, Deepali Shital Gotadke, Ranjitha S, Rama Narayanan, Srividya Puppala

Contents

Hidden History Behind the Mystery

The Neck of the Woods

Societal Constraints

The Saga of Her Start-up

Hidden History
Behind the Mystery

Meet the Editor

Oindrila Ghatak is an Indian Bengali girl who is based in the UK for work. She is passionate about writing and writes on versatile subjects. She is an engineer and a business degree holder by profession with the soul of an artist. She is someone who loves to pen down her thoughts into words. "The soul I bear finds its solace in words and art", says the bubbly girl from Kolkata. She loves to paint and mimic cartoon characters as well.

You can connect with her on Instagram @arindrila.

Editor's Note

Being a compiler and editor for the first time, I was a bit nervous on how to take this role up. I am an author but this time I was definitely excited as I wanted to try something new. And I am glad that I went forward with my decision. I got the opportunity to interact and bond with some fantastic people while working with Inkfeathers group and I am proud to be a part of this team. As I am always learning at every phase of my life, I learnt a lot from this team especially holding on to each other when things are going low. Reading and compiling these amazing pieces by my coauthors were thrilling as mystery is the genre, I have loved all my life. I genuinely thank my Inkfeathers team, be it my coauthors and anyone who contributed in making this book a success.

And to the readers, whoever is a mystery freak, this theme will give a restless urge for each story to unfold despite the anxious thrills, even sometimes leaving with open endings, keeping the thirst unclenched so that you get back into the book again and again!

~Oindrila Ghatak

1

A Tale of Two

Claire Casapao

Mud squelches under shoes.

Sobs fill the air.

An incredulous whisper of 'He can't be dead, can he?'

Melancholy violin music starts playing—it sounds like fingernails scratching a blackboard.

'He is.'

The confirmation of their worst fears hits them like a truck.

Years Ago:

The sun rises high in the sky, streaking the clouds with gold and orange.

Loud trumpet noises play.

Panting.

Shouts of 'Faster!'

A recruit lags behind the large crowd of others ahead.

He can't run any faster.

He can't run any further.

But he keeps going.

Every day, until he gets stronger.

His resolve never wavers.

Night-time:

The recruit is wide awake. He wonders who could sleep through his bunkmates' loud snoring. Certainly not him.

He thinks of his family, far away from him. He remembers his old life.

He remembers why he's there, stretched out over a bed in the barracks of the military academy.

He wants to protect his country.

The recruit is still wide awake. He sneaks down the bed, trying not to wake anyone up.

Push-ups were horrible for him. 'I'm going to change that,' he thought.

Two hundred push-ups later, the recruit decides to get some rest. Tiptoeing softly back to his bed, he trips over a loose floorboard.

'Footsteps.'

The recruit runs.

The Next Day:

'You are soldiers, not lazy rats. You must be able to endure all kinds of conditions. Most importantly, you must not give up. You are here to protect your country.'

The recruits are running once more.

This recruit is still stumbling. He's falling apart. He's sweating uncontrollably. He can't keep going. He has to stop.

He falls down.

Down, down and down.

He feels traumatized.

He feels panicked.

He'll never be able to make it. He's not good enough.

His subconscious swirls with these thoughts.

He'll never be enough. He can't do it. He has to pack up and go home and face the exultation of all those people who said he wouldn't make it.

Horrifying deprecating remarks fly through the recruit's mind. He doesn't notice anything else. He doesn't notice how much faster he runs than he used to. He doesn't notice he's starting to catch up.

But his head is spinning. He has to continue. He can't stop.

He's weak.

'Keep going, faster, faster!' yells the drill sergeant.

The recruit pulls himself out of his subconscious back into the sunshine—into the real world. He finally notices the light in what he believes to be darkness.

Last Day:

The recruit…the valedictorian. He is the best.

He has the best endurance. He is the strongest.

He has never forgotten how he used to be—the weak, stuttering, and stumbling recruit.

'Kid, why don't you become a drill sergeant?'

'I don't like yelling at people, sir.'

'Nonsense, we don't just yell at people, we motivate them.'

'I still don't want to.'

'So, you're going to join the army? You want to fight?'

'Yes, sir.'

'They need someone like you, now that they've declared war.'

The War:

The recruit is now a soldier.

Bullets are flying from all directions.

Bodies fall onto the mud, lifeless.

He didn't want to be one of them.

He fought hard and bravely for his country.

He sacrificed a normal civilian life.

He thought of this—it propelled him to keep fighting.

A bullet rushes past him and hits the soldier next to him in the chest.

The soldier shoots the opposing army's commander in the neck.

The battle was won.

'More battles.'

'More victories.'

The soldier rises through the ranks.

He becomes the general of the army.

His troops fight through the war under his leadership.

It seems as if they will emerge victorious.

Until tragedy strikes.

The Final Night of the War:

The general's body lay on the floor, still and cold, with a bullet embedded in his chest. The walls and floor were spattered with thick, dark red blood.

Those walls were the only witness to the fatal deed.

A tall man had snuck into the general's room in the middle of the night. The general had been fast asleep.

He was oblivious to the heavy footsteps approaching his bed. The tall man slowly drew a revolver out of his pocket and shot him.

The general's dead body rolled off the bed, onto the floor where it lay, silent and unmoving until sunrise.

The Morning After:

The general's soldiers found a piece of paper on his nightstand. A letter from his wife. It only contained one sentence.

'War is a living hell—end it. By that, I mean, win it.'

Present Day:

The miserable mood is infectious. 'He was a great man!' exclaims a woman passionately. 'He had a family! He had a promising career! My poor little boy,' sobs the general's mother. His widow attempts to console her.

'He's not your little boy anymore – he's grown up to be a man – a protector. He protects all of us. We have not all been wiped out yet because of his courage. We have even won the war! He died for a cause he believed in, and that's something to be proud of.'

A tall, thin black shadow appears at the gates of the cemetery. It's the general's murderer.

Meanwhile (More tragedy):

The murderer is wearing a dark cloak and hood, obscuring his features. He is carrying a revolver – the same one that killed the general.

The taste of revenge becomes sweeter as he approaches the melancholy party.

No one notices him—their tears cloud their vision. It is evident to the murderer that this will be easy—as easy as assassinating the general.

Gunshots ring through the air, one after the other. Each one is punctuated by a scream and a thud.

Soon, the murderer is facing the last person alive. The general's widow.

He slowly pulls off his hood.

He's the drill sergeant.

'Why are you doing this?' she demands.

'It's not fit for ugly little housewives like you to know my reasons,' snarled the drill sergeant.

'The phrase 'ugly little housewives' does not include me – for one, I was a spy for the military. Our military. And you know you're just jealous of my husband's success.'

'Jealous, am I?'

Flashback:

The drill sergeant is sitting in his room with the general – a recruit back then.

'Kid, why don't you become a drill sergeant?'

'I don't like yelling at people, sir.'

'Nonsense, we don't just yell at people, we motivate them.'

'I still don't want to.'

'So, you're going to join the army? You want to fight?'

'Yes, sir.'

'They need someone like you, now that they've declared war.'

'Sir, can you have a family and still be a soldier?'

'I heard that there are benefits for married soldiers in the army, only our army, to bait people into joining. Why do you ask?'

'Just asking.'

With this, the recruit gets up and returns to the barracks.

A year after this conversation, before the recruit joined the army, he married the drill sergeant's younger sister. His only sister.

For his own personal gain.

He wanted to get the benefits married soldiers did in their army. He didn't love her.

So, she joined the army as a spy. Secretly, while pretending to be a housewife, just to get closer to him.

Or so her brother thought.

Present Day:

'I hate to call you my brother,' whispered the widow, softly.

'Can't you see? He would have never loved you; You desperate, naïve brat! He was using you! I don't want to see you running around like a little dog!' he screamed.

'And I didn't join the army just to get close to him! You old bag! I wanted to protect my country, just as he did!'

The widow's patience had finally reached its end. She yanked the revolver out of her brother's hands and pointed it at him.

'Your own brother?' asks the drill sergeant, laughing.

'The brother who doesn't even know my name!' she screeches. 'The brother who insulted my family! The brother who murdered innocent people! Just because he thought I needed saving! I'm not a damsel in distress, you know! And I'm more than what you think I am! I'm stronger than you think! I'm not that little girl who sobbed uncontrollably when she fell on her face anymore!'

She pulls on the trigger.

The last gunshot had been fired.

2

Murder He GOOGOOED

Sandhita Agarwal

"Goo-Goo Gaga". That's what you expect from a baby right? I don't know if all babies can think the way I can, maybe I am one of these prodigious genius babies on the news. I wish I could tell my parents that I am smarter than them. But you see I still cannot speak. I am officially 12 months old but unofficially I have been born a very long time. I was living in the 7th dimension, but I had been bored in my world. I will tell you more about that dimension later. So, I was conceived by a lovely couple called Dick and Jane. I chose them from a catalogue. I was given the choice because I was a great phenomenon in the 7th dimension. I was a very important concept that was vital in everyday life. You could compare me to the law of gravity here in this dimension. I am sure that the concepts in this dimension also become sentient life in another dimension on Earth. Anyway, I chose Dick and Jane to be my loving parents. It was on the night of 14th June that Dick decided to get a little wild. They had been trying to get pregnant for months without fruition. Dick's Indian friend Raj took him to his ayurvedic doctor, Dr Sharma. Dr Sharma presented Dick with some roots that he was to make tea out of. Dick reluctantly brought back home the roots. How do I know all this? Because I was there! I was already born and waiting to be conceived by my parents. They don't know all this. I am sure they were born the same way or pretty much the same way but have now forgotten all of it. I think that's what happens once you start speaking. You lose the memories of the 7th dimension. I think that's what the conductor had told me before bidding me farewell.

I am not telling you all this because I want to share the secrets of the 7th dimension with you. You wouldn't believe me anyway. I want to talk about something else, something that's been weighing on my mind for the past few weeks. I saw someone being murdered. I can only imagine the trauma that my mind is going through right now. From my experience in the 7th dimension, a trauma in early childhood leads to a fragmented psyche. This is probably one of the reasons why I am telling you all this. I don't want to grow up to become a Ted Bundy or Jeffrey Dahmer.

When I entered this world, I was shocked beyond anything. Everything was so different, so unreal. My mind was processing so many inputs that it never had to deal with before. And for the first few months, I couldn't stop crying. Everything scared me because I couldn't understand so many things. For instance, before my birth in your world, I couldn't see. The sense of sight was something unrequired in my world. As were taste, speech, and hearing. The sense of touch remains quite the same. Our sense of touch was developed beyond anything that I am experiencing now. As I got used to my new senses, I started to feel more comfortable in this world. I was rather enjoying my time in this world, until the night of the murder.

A story is like a many-headed demon, to banish it you must catch one of its heads and then start with your exorcism. My story begins on 24th February, exactly 2 months after my birth. Jane, my mother, was exhausted from the sleepless nights. I was keeping her busy with my constant hunger. Hunger was also something new for me. The taste of my mother's breast milk was a revelation. I couldn't get enough of that thing. I could see the effect of my constant needs affecting her. But I couldn't help it. I needed her till I got used to this new world. From the pictures, I could see that my mother had been a beautiful woman. For me, beauty is a concept that has transformed in this world. My mind is slowly wrapping its head around the way my eyes see beauty. My mother had long brown hair, green eyes, and a beautiful warm smile. The last two months had made her weak and sleepless. But I knew she was happy inside. She loved me with a force that has now made me love her in turn. This woman who birthed me, this woman who loves me more than she loves herself.

On the night of February 24th, my father returned home from his role as a Senior VP in a big tech firm. He was a tall, handsome man with a voice that I later learned blew the panties off of women. I had chosen these people to be my parents and one of the reasons was their high ranking in this world. I will not explain how we ranked the beings of this world, but it was a combination of moral fibre, past lives, and present societal status.

The next month passed in a blur of breasts, poops, and sleeping. I wanted to know more about this world and my curiosity and fears were becoming annoying. But my physical body was still weak, and I needed nutrition and sleep. I was a selfish baby clinging to my mother 24 hours a day. There was something about her that soothed my anxiety. On the 4th day of the 4th month of my existence here, my father brought a drink in a pretty shiny bottle with a golden cap at the end. My mother was in the kitchen preparing his dinner. I was playing peek-a-boo with Rita. When my mother saw the bottle, she shouted "Champagne". And leapt into my dad's arms. From the conversation that ensued, I realised my dad had gotten a promotion at work and had been made the president of the company. My father talked about having a lot of people working under him and new executive powers. My parents seemed very happy and that made me happy. That night was the first that my parents left me with Rita and were holed up in their room for a few hours. I tried my best to not miss my mother, but it was pointless. I cried for her, but she didn't come. Rita tried to soothe me by hugging me. But Rita didn't smell like my mother, and it didn't comfort me. I felt betrayed. I felt angry. I resolved not to stop crying till my mother came to me. And she did after I was almost blue from crying. I am ashamed to say I felt relieved. My dad followed my mom with an irritated look in his eyes and I smirked at him. It gave me immense happiness to see that my mother had chosen me over him.

That incident scared me. I swore to not let my mother out of my sight ever again. Looking back, I can see how miserable I made her. But I don't know what happened to me at that time. I just couldn't stay away from her even for a moment. By the time I was 6 months old, I understood more about my mother and her needs. I was settling down into my body and I decided to give my mother a bit of rest. I let my nanny Rita take care of me while my mother started her job hunting. My father was often very late from work, and we hardly saw him anymore. His dinners would go uneaten, saved in plastic Tupperware for the next day, and then thrown into the compost bin. My mother started going out for longer periods of time and leaving me alone with Rita. I tried to be a good baby. And even though I missed her a lot, she would be back before I got up fed and started crying. She seemed happier and had started looking more like her photographs on the walls. It made me happy to see my mother radiant again.

As I hit my 8th month, my mother found a job as a senior android developer in a food delivery company. My father came home early that day with a paper bag full of food: from her favourite Mexican restaurant, Tareo. The first time I tasted their guacamole I almost died of ecstasy. My mother had made a video of my reaction and uploaded it to YouTube as "Baby's reaction to Guacamole". I had received over 100,000 views in 2 months. Yes, I am a famous baby. Since then whenever I smell that tart guacamole smell, I cry. I cry for that mushy delicious thing that makes my tastebuds dance. I imagine my tastebuds dancing like the Teletubbies I watch on TV. I like the Teletubbies. They look fat and cute, and they dance. I would like to dance too. But my motor skills are not yet fully developed. We all sat around the focal point in any family's life, the tv, and ate; me sitting in my highchair and my mom feeding me tiny spoonfuls of guac with small bites of cerelac in between, and my father on the sofa, watching the news munching on some tacos. I have often demanded tacos and burritos from my mother, but she simply doesn't understand me. I tell her to give them to me, I can handle them, and I know she can feel my requests, yet chooses to look up the answers on her phone, shaking her head and pronouncing that I was too young for such delicacies. I was a happy child cocooned in the love and warmth of my family.

I remember the weekends being extra special for me. My mom and dad would both wake up to a lazy day. They often stayed home making special breakfasts and watching movies. Sometimes they would take me out for lunch or dinner. They would sit talking to each other for hours and their love filled me with such a joy that I cannot describe.

My mother started working the next week and left me alone with Rita. I wanted to be mature about it. I wanted to be a good baby for my mother. But it hurt. I missed my mother so much. It was like a physical ache in my body, an ache centred somewhere in my tummy. The first time she left me, I was confused. I had heard her talking about starting work, but I had not fully understood what that meant. I waited for her that day. Rita tried to feed me cereal which I usually liked. But I refused. She then brought a bottle and stuck it in my reluctant mouth. I liked the flavour of that. It tasted like my mom's milk. Now that I have seen my mom leave her milk in the bottle every day using some kind of hydraulic machine, I drink it eagerly. It helps me connect to my mom in her absence. I was crying the first day when I saw my mom's car drive into the garage. She usually took me to the shopping centre in it. I started bawling even more because I wanted to show her how unhappy I had been. My mom rushed inside and picked me up. I cried a bit more for good measure and then let her soothe me with her cooing voice. Every time she tried to put me down, I cried. I know I was being mean, but I just needed to be with her. I didn't see my dad that day.

Her absence during the day became a routine. It hurt every day, but the pain got duller with each passing week. Rita was good with me. She told me stories of princes and princesses and of a man called Stephen

Hawking. I liked her tales because they helped me understand the new world a bit more every day. Rita was a thin girl of about 24 years. She had blonde hair and large, kind brown eyes. From her conversations on the phone, I knew Rita's boyfriend was far away in the military. I don't know what that word means yet. I know Rita wants to get married to him soon. The concept of marriage is familiar to me. Beings in the 7th dimension mate for life. I sometimes miss my mate. We cannot reproduce because we are concepts. Or were concepts? I also know that Rita has a secret.

The first time my mother started talking to me about her problems was when I was in my 10th month. My father was still at the office and Rita had gone back home. My mother and I were alone in the kitchen. I was in my highchair, anticipating the smells emanating from my mother's cooking. I was not a fussy baby, on the contrary, I had the desire to taste and consume. My mental curiosity matched the curiosity of my taste buds. My mother sat down next to me and fed me my first mouthful of a white and brown substance which now I know were rice and beans. The textures of the food amazed me. I loved it. The saltiness of the beans and their mushy yet firm texture. Rice is the best vehicle for any kind of food. As I was enjoying my meal, my mother started talking about her rather long and tough workday; about the database crash that had happened after she pushed a new feature to the server; how she had combed through her code looking for the bug; how embarrassed she had been in front of her manager; how scared she had been the whole time the other engineers had been going through her code; how she had finally found the tiny mistake; an empty if loop. I listened with rapt attention. Everything was new to me, but I understood it. I am good at absorbing the concepts in any conversation and using my new tools to envisage that concept. I could also sense the loneliness coming off in waves from my mother. I think she needed someone to hold her and make her feel safe, the way daddy used to do. But he wasn't there at that moment. At that moment I was afraid. I could sense darkness on the horizon. We finished our dinners and my mother put me to bed. By that time, I had learned to be a good baby and follow a schedule. When my mother thought I was asleep, I saw her sobbing softly into her pillow. I saw her dialling my dad and talking to him. She sounded angry. I wanted to reach out to her and comfort her the way my dad always did. But I couldn't. My mother got up from her bed and quietly went out of the room. She returned with a glass of red liquid, (now I know red wine), the liquid that will become her companion on rough nights.

That weekend, we planned our first getaway after my birth. Daddy had booked flights to a place called Hawaii. My mother was the happiest I had seen in weeks. Rita was also coming with us. My family's excitement was infectious. I was eager to explore the world outside of my house and the park where Rita usually took me. The day of the departure was approaching, and the house was bustling. My mom packed her favourite dresses into her black suitcase. I woke up the day before the departure to find my mom and dad yelling at each other in the kitchen. I was scared and started crying. My mother soon appeared at the door and picked me up. There was a loud boom of my dad closing the door and then the sounds of his car engines turning. My mother started crying after this. The house had turned into an orchestra of mother and baby crying. The sight of my mother crying sent me into a panic attack. If she was crying who was going to soothe me? My mother soon regained her composure and fetched my milk bottle. I slowly started feeling better. She set me down in the highchair and called my grandmother. I was shocked to learn that daddy had cancelled the vacation because he had an important meeting coming up that day. But there was more to the story. My mother was talking about smelling someone else on daddy's breath. Her womanly instincts were alarmed, and she was confused. At that time, I did not fully understand the implications of her words and I was as confused as she was.

Daddy didn't return the following day. My mother was worried. She kept calling grandma. Daddy did return the next day and there was a lot of drama in the kitchen. Daddy brought my mother a large diamond ring and hugged her till she cried. They left me alone that night with Rita and went somewhere. I knew that I had to be a good baby and didn't cry. I woke up in the morning to see my mother happy and radiant.

It was 24 days before my first birthday that I knew I would never be happy again. It was the day that would set the theme for my life. The day had started like any other day. Mom goes off to work and Rita took me for a walk in the park. My mom came back and got Mexican food. I was thrilled. My mom was just putting me to bed when dad came home, early for the first time in months. He went straight to the bathroom for a shower while my mom gathered his clothes to put for laundry. I think that's when she noticed the long blonde hair on his coat. I don't think she thought too much about it. I know of this because she spoke about it to grandma the next day. But something sank deep within my heart. It was a premonition of the things to come. Over the next few days, I could feel my mother on edge. She was always tense like something was about to happen. Her moods affected me. My stomach started getting upset. I would burp and hiccup the whole day. And Rita would try to pat my back and alleviate my condition.

On Sunday, when my dad went into the kitchen to get more popcorn, I saw my mom quickly pick up his phone and do something to it. After a few minutes of tinkering, she quickly put it back in its place. The next day, my mom did something she had not done in months, she didn't go to work. I heard her talk to her boss about taking the day off. She then opened her laptop and started doing something. I was in my crib with a bottle in my mouth. I wanted to tell my mom, 'No! Don't do it! DO NOT DO IT!' but I couldn't. I saw her expressions change from those of anticipation and anxiety to ones of shock. Her hand went up to her mouth as she felt her whole world shatter. I cannot say I was shocked. I had often heard my dad's whispered conversations with the other woman when my mom was downstairs in the kitchen. The next day my mom left me at my grandmother's. I don't know what happened, but I am guessing that she confronted my dad. My mother picked me up in the evening. Dad was waiting for us at home. He hugged me and kissed me. He cooked dinner for mom that night and we lay in the warm glow of the television.

The next day was my first birthday and my parents had organized a huge party. They had been planning it for weeks. The invites were sent out, the caterers called, and the hall was booked. My mother had bought me a very smart navy-blue suit with a matching top hat. I was looking forward to wearing that.

Evening rolled in and everybody got ready. I looked at myself in the suit and I am sorry to say I looked really fine, like a young handsome prince. I had planned to woo everybody in the hall by walking for the first time. I had been walking on my own for the past few days, practising till I got it right. I wanted to give my parents a surprise of my own. We all got into my dad's Lexus and made it to the venue. I was amazed by the decorations. Lots of balloons, lots of ribbons, lots of food. My mother kissed me over and over as we waited for their friends to arrive. Soon the hall was filled with lots of people and the noise of it all made my head hurt a bit. I was waiting to give my performance. There was music and my mother handed me over to my dad as she joined a few of her friends in dancing. She was a great dancer. I watched her in amazement as she moved to the beats. 'Oh! Oh!' I thought. I had made a poopoo in my pants. My dad suddenly scrunched up his face when he realized what I had done. He started looking for my diapers in the baby bag my mom had packed. But he couldn't find any. He tried calling out to my mother, but she was lost in her rhythm. My dad smiled and I think he wanted to let her enjoy the night. I wished he had called her. I wished there were diapers in the bag. I wished my dad had not decided to go home to get some diapers. However, I find myself directly responsible for what happened next. If only I had chosen another time to release my bowels, maybe, just maybe I could have prevented the incident that ruined our lives.

My dad placed me in the child seat and tightened the seat belts. He got into the car, and we drove away to our house, which was a mere 10 minutes away. He got out of the car, picked me up, and brought me inside the house. We were upstairs in the walk-in closet when the doorbell rang. My dad put me down in the crib and went downstairs. Something wasn't right, I knew that. Noises were coming from downstairs. I climbed out of my crib as I had done many times before and stood at the top of the stairs looking down at them. My dad and his killer. They were having a heated argument. The killer then pulled something out of its coat, something black and shiny. I knew it was a weapon, something that extinguished the lives of people. The killer shot my dad once in the stomach and once in the face. A part of my dad's face exploded into tiny red pieces that got stuck to the walls and the balustrade. The killer saw me and pointed the gun at me. I knew the killer and I knew that they wouldn't shoot me. The killer then quickly ran out the door. I stood at the top of the stairs looking at the red mess downstairs, marvelling at the deep red, the richness of the end. A sudden feeling overcame me, and everything went black.

My mom was sobbing softly into a pillow when I woke up. She looked at me and hope returned to her eyes. I had large tubes in my mouth and my head hurt. My mom's mother was also in the room with us. The doctor was called to the room. The doctor told my mom that I would be ok. She wept with joy. As I would understand later, I had fallen from the top of the stairs to the landing 4 stairs down. I had been saved from grave injuries because of the flush carpeting on the stairs.

We were staying at grandma's till the police finished their investigation. I don't know how the police here work. But two people came to question my mother and grandparents. There was a tall, dark policeman who was called Bailey by the other man. Bailey was scary. He had grim eyes and a thin-lipped mouth that never smiled. The other man was a short paunchy fellow. I don't know his name, but his eyes had a certain sadness to them that I had never seen before. The short man gave me a doughnut when he first saw me. My mother smiled at him, but he didn't smile back at her. I heard them talk about the night of the party. How my mother had excused herself to go to the restroom and hadn't been seen by anyone for more than an hour. My mother then showed them a text that she had received at that time. A text that had said,' Your husband is here with me now, come see us how we play, while you and your son celebrate, we roll around naked in the hay and then an address. My mother had been furious and had left the party to go to an apartment complex 20 minutes away in her car. She went to the unit number and rang the bell. Nobody opened the door. She then tried to peep in through the windows. Everything was dark inside. She tried calling the number, but it was unreachable. She then got back into her car and came back to the party. Dick was still not at the party, so she came back home with grandma to look for him and me. That's when they found dad dead and I passed out. The police confiscated her phone and asked her not to leave the city. My mom looked shocked.

My dad's funeral was held the next week. I saw the killer there weeping like everyone else, just another bereaved person. It has been two weeks since my dad's murder. My mom cries all the time. I have nightmares of the killer coming to kill me. I know the killer would never hurt me. But I am still afraid. I want to tell someone who the real killer is, but I am afraid. I see my dad in my dreams sometimes. The three of us having lunch at Tareo's but then suddenly there would be a boom, and half of my dad's face would be gone. And we would still sit there having food while my dad looked at me with only one eye, trying to smile with the red flesh gaping at me from his wounds. I cry often now, and nothing soothes me anymore. Not even my mother's touch.

3

Loyal-Tea

Aanika Gajendragad

It was a sunny afternoon in Goa and dining in Alberto's restaurant with the Calangute beach in view felt like paradise. His place was known for his cotton candy ice cream, and because it was summer his business flourished. Customers gushed about the *vindaloo* (a very hot and spicy curry) he made. He walked around hurriedly, serving the customers with all his passion. His restaurant was spacious. It even had an outdoor place to eat, decorated with creepers. But the restaurant wouldn't go a day without getting filled.

He heard a bell ring, indicating someone had come. Alberto had tied a bell to the door, so he knew when someone entered his restaurant. 'Welcome to my restaurant. Thank you for coming.' He smiled at the foreigners and gestured to the only free table in the room.

'What would you like to order?' He asked them.

The one that seemed older said something in a foreign language Alberto assumed was Japanese. He tilted his head, looking at the other girl for help.

'Um, she's asking for the Oshibori. It's a hot towel given to clean our hands with at the start of every meal. It's mom's first time out of Japan,' the girl explained.

'Right. I'll get it.'

'You don't have to,' she said.

'No, I must serve my customers well. I'll be right back.' He went inside and returned with the towel, the customers thanked him.

Just then the bell rang again, only this time it wasn't a customer. 'Xavier. It's been a long. How have you been?' Alberto asked the man who had entered. He had a paintbrush on his ear, the one where you get to know he's a painter even if you don't know him.

'Alberto, my good old friend. I have come to give you a gift,' the man whispered.

'There's no occasion today, is there?'

'Does it have to be an occasion to give my dear friend a gift?' He embraced Alberto.

'No, what is it?' Alberto's eyes travelled to the canvas he was holding. Xavier handed it over. It was a painting of Alberto serving his customers. 'When did you draw this?' Asked Alberto, surprised.

'Oh, just a few days back. Do you like it?'

'I'm gonna hang it right there,' he answered, pointing to the wall of paintings.

'I'm glad you liked it, Berto. Now that you have taken it, I don't have any business here. I shall leave.'

'Have some tea before you leave,' Alberto suggested.

'Maybe another day, your restaurant is full now,' he smiled and walked away. Alberto was about to insist but a customer at a table called him over, and yet again, he had to choose his job over his customer-turned-friend.

'Did you hear?' He heard someone say when he was handing out the menu to another customer. 'Hear what?' the other asked.

'About Francisca?' The first said. Alberto's ears perked.

'What about her?'

'You didn't hear? Her neighbour says she died,' she continued.

'I'm sorry to have overheard you, who did you say died?' Alberto couldn't help but ask.

'Francisca Fernandes, why? Do you know her?' The woman replied.

'I do, as a matter of fact. She was a regular customer.' He hung his head low.

'Really, well then I'm sorry for your loss,' she breathed. The two paid the bill and rushed out before Alberto could ask for more. He let out a big sigh before continuing his work.

Fransisca was a foodie. The whole of her family was. She always ate in restaurants because she loved the food they cooked, or so she claimed. Everyone believed it was because she didn't know how to cook. Her parents ordered food home and seldom went out to dine. They were connoisseurs of food. Of wine, more like. They loved to drink and even knew everything about wines.

~~~

Inspector Shirodkar fixed his glasses, flipping through pages every now and then.

'Who is the inspector? Tell me! We won't leave until this case is solved,' someone shouted from outside. He looked up to find two angry people- a middle-aged couple- storming into his room. 'What's the matter?' The inspector queried.

'Inspector, our daughter...she-she died. But we're sure there isn't any kind of disease or problem she had, she was physically fit.' The man complained.

'And mentally,' the woman added.

'Are you sure it wasn't a suicide?' He asked the parents.

'I know my child. She would never do this,' the mother looked offended.

'Okay, we shall examine the body.'

The inspector grimly nodded before gesturing for them to leave his cabin.

'A poisonous medicine inside the victim's body without her going
~~~

out anywhere on the day of her death. That's very unusual.' He thought to himself.

'Did you check where Fransisca went the previous day?' the Inspector questioned one of the policemen.

'She didn't go anywhere, sir. She was home the whole day,' the police answered.

'What about the day before?'

'She went to Falerio's for breakfast and Alberto's for lunch, sir.'

'Really. Summon Falerio for interrogation.'

'And Alberto?'

'Bring Falerio first.' The policeman scurried away. The inspector and Alberto were really good friends. Alberto was friends with everyone, but the bond between these two was different. Shirodkar loved him like a brother. So did Alberto. The inspector knew him very well. He knew Alberto's care for his customers and that he could never think of murder.

On the other hand, Falerio was like a hooligan. He sold drugs in his restaurant without the knowledge of the authorities. Well, you could call it an open secret. He had dark circles around his eyes and messy hair; he barely spoke to anyone. Yet the food he cooked was good enough to attract many customers. He was as famous as Alberto in the state.

When the policemen had brought Falerio inside, he didn't try to defend himself. He was silent. They took him to the huge white room in which Shirodkar sat, ready to interrogate him.

'So Falerio, do you know who Fransisca Fernandes is?'

'She might have come to my restaurant many times, yes,' Falerio admitted.

'Do you know about her passing?'

'I didn't know. That's terrible,' he said. The inspector eyed him suspiciously.

'It is. The doctor says it's because of a drug inside her body that killed her.'

Falerio nodded.

'You're not denying it to be you,' he pointed out.

'What's the use, you'll arrest me anyway.'

'So, it is you.'

'You do your duty, and if you have proof, you can arrest me. In any which ways, I will not force-feed my customers,' Falerio said firmly.

'Did Fransisca come to your restaurant two days back?'

'She did.'

'We'll check what she ordered, then.' He stood.

'My restaurant's all yours.'

The two, along with a few other policemen, went to the restaurant. Falerio opened the list of orders on his computer. 'She ordered an omelette. No drinks,' Inspector motioned to the policeman next to him to note it down. 'Where's the CCTV?'

Falerio guided them to a room. There wasn't anything suspicious on the CCTV though. Fransisca simply came, ate, paid and left.

'Hmm. We'll be keeping an eye on you. Do not leave the city without our permission.'

'Sir, the drug can't be chewed. I would suggest you interrogate Alberto too,' said the doctor, Maria.

'We need a solid ground for interrogating a gentleman like Alberto,' Shirodkar seemed unconcerned.

'I am aware of that, but just-'

'I like your zeal, just in two years you've shown your worth,' Shirodkar interrupted with a backhanded compliment.

It was true. Maria had just started her job as a doctor, 3-4 years ago. This was her first important case. She wanted to know who killed Fransisca, and why they'd do such a thing. She knew what she reported would most likely not be correct, of course, who knew better than an experienced Inspector having worked for over 30 years? But this time she was sure it wouldn't be Falerio. Her instincts told her so. She didn't find anything wrong in questioning Alberto.

'Are you not suspecting Alberto because he's a good friend? I can file a suit against that,' she joked hesitantly.

'That's merely not the reason. I've known him almost my whole life. He hasn't once done anything bad. He was that silent kid in school too. I won't suspect him because I know it isn't him.'

'Sir-'

'That's the end of the discussion.' He left.

But Maria wouldn't give up that easily. She decided she would go to Alberto's herself to question the man.

And that's what she did. The next day, she set off to solve the mystery. She was known for her espionage skills when she was young. She always read mystery books then. She knew a tip to find them in the huge libraries too, the mystery books had black pages on the outside.

'Alberto, right?' She smiled at the tall guy in front of her.

'That's me. What would you like to order?' He replied.

'Actually, do you mind if I check your list of orders? I have something I need to prove.' She clenched her jaw.

'Oh. Do you mind if I ask who you are and what you need to prove?'

'I'm Doctor Maria. I'm sorry I can't tell-' she started. 'Oh well, it's about Fransisca.' She said. She wanted to see Alberto's reaction to the mention of her name.

'M-maria, you say?' She was sure she heard him stutter. 'Sure. Follow me.' Within a second he remained calm and led the way.

'She ordered a Burger and tea, eh? Could you give me some tea too?'

'Of course.'

He set to prepare the tea while Maria sat to think. She saw him texting someone from the corner of her eye.

'Tea...could he have used it? But it was two days before the death. I don't know any kind of drug that kills two days later.'

Alberto came back with the tea in hand. 'Here.'

'Thank you.'

She took a sip and it tasted normal. It tasted very good, to be honest. There wasn't anything wrong with it. Thousands of people drink it every day, the same tea. But what grudge could Alberto have had against Fransisca?

She received a message from Inspector Shirodkar just then.

'Do not think too much, Maria. We don't know if it is Alberto yet.'

She went to Fransisca's parents' house to ask about Alberto and Fransisca's relationship. 'Oh, there was no personal relationship at all. She was just a regular customer there and he was really nice to her all the time,' they answered.

'I see. Thank you.' Then she returned to the police station.

'Sir, as I told you, the drug can't be chewed. But Fransisca didn't drink anything at Falerio's. She did at Alberto's,' Maria said to Shirodkar.

'That is a very lame reason, Maria. Falerio might have put the drug in the omelette.'

'That isn't possible, sir. After the post-mortem, we found an indigestible capsule cover in her intestine. She would've choked then and there if she ate it.'

'How didn't she choke when she drank it, then?' He was now interested.

'The drug, I observed, could be swallowed and not chewed.'

'Yeah? How do I know you're not lying?' He came closer.

'I can show it to you.'

'Why are you bringing me here? Leave me, let me go!' Alberto was the opposite of Falerio, who was silent.

'Alberto. Hello,' the inspector cleared his throat.

'I can't believe you're suspecting your dear friend of ages now,' Alberto sounded hurt.

'Was it you?' Shirodkar interrogated.

'No! It wasn't me. Do you think I would do such a thing?'

'I don't know, Alberto. Just please be honest.'

Alberto sat silent.

'Answer me.'

'I told you it wasn't me,' he growled.

'Okay then. Let's check the CCTV, shall we?'

'No! I mean, I don't have a CCTV.'

'We both know that isn't true,' Shirodkar shook his head.

'What if I say it was me? Would you kill me?'

'We would arrest you, that's for sure. Is it you?'

Alberto remained silent.

The police decided to check the surveillance meanwhile.

'Sir, we sent the clip to you,' one of them said to the inspector.

He pressed play with shaky hands. In it, Alberto served tea to her. She was busy talking on the phone and didn't pay attention to the tea. When she had finished drinking it, she coughed a little before leaving. The CC camera caught him smirking after she had left.

When the video had ended, Shirodkar looked up to see Alberto sobbing.

'Mind explaining?' Shirodkar couldn't believe his very own friend could do such a thing.

'It was me. I killed her. I had to. Fransisca didn't only eat at my competitor's place, but also came to my restaurant and praised him in front of the customers.'

'Who is your competitor?' The inspector asked. Alberto sighed and looked at Falerio with guilty eyes.

'What…' Shirodkar's voice came out squeaky. 'What kind of drug did you give her?'

'It's called the DATD.'

'Right. We need to arrest you.'

'I know.' Alberto hung his head again, this time genuinely sad.

'Thank you so much, doctor and inspector,' the parents said.

'It was all her.' The inspector nudged Maria.

'I knew it all along,' she held her head high.

'But how did you figure out it was him?' Shirodkar asked.

'I had to do a bit of a psychological study for this one. He was really passionate about his job and served his customers well when I saw him yesterday. I then researched. It's called the Othello syndrome, what he has. He was jealous of Falerio. Which led to murder,' she expressed.

~~~

'Wow- how did you cook up that story in 10 minutes?' My friend asked me.

'I have talent.' I flipped my hair.

'That's a pretty good story for a fifteen-year-old. One thing I didn't understand, what's DATD?'

'Couldn't you guess? It's the short form of 'Die After Two Days.' I laughed.

'Oh, haha! Another thing, I don't know how you can swallow a pill in tea without knowing,' she said, eyeing me while I finished my cold tea.
~~~

4

Murder in Ahuja Apartments

Aditya Jhingan

It was 8 in the morning, and nobody would have thought about such a horrifying incident.

Ahuja Apartments just witnessed its first bloody murder. An elderly couple in their 80s Mr & Mrs Kumar were brutally murdered. Shot in the middle of their heads.

It was a very pleasant day for the couple since it was Mrs Kumar's birthday. Mr Sanjay Kumar surprised his wife Mrs Lalita Kumar with a gorgeous-looking bouquet, and a very ravishing gold beaded pearl necklace. Mrs Kumar was very excited; her peaceful morning began with such wonderful gifts and love from her husband.

As she indulged in her morning chores, her husband came and sat in the living room and started reading the newspaper. A few moments later both were sipping on hot tea and discussing how they are going to spend their day, by making a list. In the meanwhile, they heard a noise of a click as in someone trying to unlock the door. (A voice that even a dog could get suspicious of.)

With a fast pace, Mr Kumar checked on his front door asking, 'Who's there?' while opening the door, a hand with a handkerchief in a quick action landed on his face making him feel dizzy within a few seconds he fainted as the killer caught him, placing him on the floor quietly. While Mrs Kumar managed to get herself up from the tea table and place the cup down. As her head turned towards the door, an iron rod came at full force and hit her head, making her lose control and she collapsed on the tea table, with the blood dripping from her skull the killer managed to slide her body down on the floor.

The killer walked towards the entrance to lock the door, and very tidily he dragged Mr Kumar to where Mrs Kumar was, near the tea table. He then took out his pistol, attached a silencer, and shot both of them right in the middle of their heads. He wasn't quite done, got down on his knees and, started punching Mr Kumar's face ferociously. He didn't stop until his face was turned into mashed potato. As for Mrs Kumar, he sliced her throat. The killer then walked into the room took off his mask and gloves, changed his clothes and washed off the blood from his fists and face. Leaving the bathroom, he set fire to that bouquet and threw it into the sink. Then he snatched that pearl necklace from the jewellery box.

Very tidily he picked up the keys with a handkerchief and locked the door on his way out. With the guard missing, he managed to place those keys on his table and exited the colony's main gate without signing the visitor's entry book.

'This is my story, what is yours?' All this has happened, and I am 95% sure, it could be someone with a very disturbing past or could be a psychopath, I need to run some tests before any more judgments, said special detective and criminal profiler, Detective Ajay Chaudhary, while staring at the crime scene.

He was the best at plotting a crime scene's rough sketch in his mind and presenting it with hard evidence which answered questions like how it could have taken place and what the nature of the killer was while doing it and what the murder weapon was.

Ajay! 'What's your analysis?' asked Senior Officer Yashwant Dutt.

Well, the killer wasn't a professional but trying to play his part, judging it's his first attempt since there hasn't been any murder in this neighbourhood. Also, since it was his first kill, he managed to kill them both and put their bodies together as a sign that could mean they did something together or sent us a message. He even left his bloodied clothes and mask, which indicates that he's an amateur.

The real question is, why such hatred against Mr Kumar only when he could have just destroyed both of their faces? He only severed her vocal cord. Also, what made him leave his clothes, 'The bloodied', clothes behind?

Assumptions are, Mr Kumar might have done something very upsetting to this smart and impatient killer of ours. And Mrs Kumar probably has said something to him.

'Anything else Officer Dutt.'

'Don't compliment the bad guy,' Ajay and no thank you.

Why don't you wrap your observations and head back to the Saint Tabitha Germane Medical Centre for Autopsy? While I'll knock some doors down.

'Yes boss,' Ajay replied while walking out of the room.

Officer Yashwant started investigating the murder by questioning the neighbours.

'Room No.9, Mrs & Mr Pathak, where were you both when all of this was taking place, right next to your walls? I am sure you might have heard something or even a whisper.' Asked officer Yashwant Pointing at the Tv wall.

'No sir, Officer we haven't heard anything, we were sleeping, we didn't even hear a glass breaking. We got in bed late last night actually we were at a colleague's house it was his birthday. So we came around 2 in the morning,' replied Mrs Pathak with sweat on her eyebrows.

'Wow!' Quite impressive, how much of deep sleepers are you both and I mean both of you. Anyway, since you both were out let me have that colleague's name and address, we will find out something at least.

Can you tell me, how Mr & Mrs Kumar were in nature, I mean how they were with others, and did they have any enemies or any family feuds?

No sir officer no enemy, no family problems, they both were very cultured and sophisticated. Even very disciplined in fact I would see a list every time they both would go out shopping.

You know Mrs Pathak in mostly all the murder investigations, probably the victims who are so innocent aren't really innocent. You see I tend to believe we all have secrets. Some are just well hidden, and some aren't.

Don't go anywhere until this crime is resolved and if we feel like we might revisit you again. Have a lovely day ahead.

Exiting the apartment, Officer Yashwant with flicking his lighter in one hand and a hat in another.

'Sir should we go with their story on the deceased and their whereabouts?' asked head constable Rathi, a baton in his hand and a notepad in another.

'Rathi ji! I never trust anyone unless they beg me with evidence. Get your busy schedule cleared, and check on their colleague, whether they were actually at that colleague's or not. Also, see what that security guard has to say, I'll head to the coroner's office for the autopsy report and 'you report back to me ASAP ordering,' officer Yashwant while getting into the police jeep.

Saint Tabitha Germane Medical Centre:

'What's the verdict doctor Mehta?' asked officer Yashwant while chewing his favourite gum.

Dr Mehta pointing towards Ajay, 'just the way Ajay described both of them shot with a pistol attached with a silencer but a very rare and new kind of pistol which isn't even registered in our database also seems to be illegal Borne 556 .9mm'.

As I can recall, this gun is very small in size. One can hide it in his pocket and still could get away with it. Even last year I witnessed a case related to this same pistol fortunately, it wasn't a murder. Anyway, let's focus on this one, so with Mrs Kumar, our killer severely damaged the internal jugular vein, which is a major blood vessel that drains blood from important body organs and parts, such as the brain, face, and neck. If not provided with immediate medical help one could die within a minute. And precisely used a very sharp knife, just like a chef's knife.

As in Mr Kumar's scene, a very specific amount of chloroform has been used to make him pass out instantly. Also, his face is partially destroyed, as per the other half, so far, I can tell his jaw is broken like the killer used his rage rather than his brain in controlling his fists.

'So the killer could be someone who has access to drugs like chloroform since it is hard to purchase any without a proper prescription. Could be someone from the medical field. What about the clothes and footprint we found Doctor at the crime scene?' asked Officer Yashwant while flicking his lighter.

Oh yes, yes how can I forget that, well I found some very interesting detail about that, the shirt is size 42 and I found traces of mud on it like our killer tripped over something and fell before reaching the crime scene and that same mud must be on his shoes, shoe size is 8 as far as I can tell, this type of mud is only found near beaches with red dust on it, just like red clay brick. Now, there is one more thing which might make your case easier, is the blood I examined in those gloves is O– so our killer is of O– blood group. Also, it seems like the entire scene took place around 6:30 to 7:30 in the morning.

'Our killer is someone who has access to drugs, legal access, he is of O– blood group, wears a size 8 in shoes, and probably someone who lives near a beach.' Officer Yashwant, while grabbing a marker and started noting down important points to catch the killer.

Sir, sir! came running down Rathi ji,

'I had a word with the guard he said, he said he saw no one but—'

'Was he asleep during his job, interrupted Officer Yashwant?'

'No, sir. He said around 6:40 am he noticed Arun Sharma entered the building with his friend, but Arun left after 10 minutes.'

Arun Sharma! 'Who the hell is this fella, and what did you find out from Mr and Mrs Pathak's colleague?' Asked Officer Yashwant.

'He is the nephew of the deceased sir and yes Mr and Mrs Pathak were at their colleague's birthday party.' Responded Rathi ji.

'Let's pay a visit to this Arun Sharma, Ajay you are with me and Rathi ji why don't you go and see if there are any beaches nearby the building where red clay bricks are made and also take the picture of that gun from Doctor Mehta, and look around in the nearest illegal weapons store or traders who supply these types of weapons. You can also take our new interns with you Nishant and Divya for your investigation and help.' Giving orders to Officer Yashwant to everyone.

Officer Yashwant and Ajay at Arun Sharma's house:

Doorbell rang!

'Where is Arun?' flicking his lighter and asking in his hoarse voice officer Yashwant.

'What is this, who are you people?' asked bluntly Mrs Sharma, Arun's mother.

While slamming the door on to the cops, Ajay stuck his foot in between.

'We are from the Police, and this is about a murder, Arun is a suspect in it, and we are just trying to investigate, please try to understand us.' Said Ajay politely.

Mrs Sharma opened the door and asked for their badges.

Do you know Mr and Mrs Kumar? asked Ajay.

Yes! I do Why? What happened to Sanjay, he's my brother. Asking worriedly and anxiously Mrs Sharma.

They are no more; I am sorry about this, and they have been brutally murdered. We suspect that your son Arun has something to do with this. Can you please call him?

'What! Arun! No, he is a great kid!' He loved his *mama ji* (uncle). Said Mrs Sharma crying and speaking with Ajay.

'Can you call him, please? We also have other angles to rectify,' said Officer Yashwant angrily.

'Arun! Arun! Come outside fast. Two officers are here to ask for you.'

'What mom? Where's the fire? And who are these two?'

'Morning Arun we are officers, and we are here to ask you some questions about your *mama ji*.' Said Ajay.

'I want a lawyer before any of your stupid questions,' shouted Arun.

'Kid, you don't know me, if it wasn't for your mom crying for you, I would drag you to the lock-up and ask you my way. You better open your mouth and with some manners.' Staring and flicking his lighter at a fast-paced, officer Yashwant.

'Leave my premises this instant before I call my lawyer', shouted Arun.

'Fine', we will come back later, replied Ajay hurriedly.

Walking out of the door, Officer Yashwant gave Arun an eerie look. He ordered Ajay to stay put here and watch if that kid does something.

In the Evening (5:00 PM):

Ajay noticed Arun step out of his house with a nervous and worried face. He was talking to someone on his phone and was carrying a backpack. He then started following Arun.

After a few moments later he noticed he is walking towards the slum area, and he specifically walked straight into the butcher shop.

Ajay immediately informed Officer Yashwant. While he was on his way out of the shop, Arun noticed 'a gum stuck to his shoe' (someone was following him). He started gushing like the wind and Ajay was left with no choice but to take out his personal pistol and alarm Arun.

By the time Officer Yashwant got there, Arun was on his knees drowned in his sorrow and tears. When questioned by the police many things came to light.

'Since childhood, they have treated me like I have been their servant, never stopped, always with the orders, they would even cuss about dad and mom in front of me. Comments like my parents were nothing but poor and failures just like me and would always act as if they care about them in front of others. You can ask mom and dad, but they would deny all of this because they were more than parents to them. And many times, *mama ji* (Mr Kumar) used to thrash dad with a stick, and he wouldn't even say anything. But I couldn't bear how they treated all three of us. Even *Mami ji* (Mrs Kumar) would never appreciate my mom for anything in fact she would always point out something wrong in everything that she does,' confessed Arun.

'So you killed them both or you hired someone for this job'? Asking Ajay staring at him.

No, I asked my friend's elder brother, who has contacts in this line of work. He introduced me to a guy named Raghu. And as for money, he gave me some time to pay him in instalments. As a matter of fact that bag I gave him had my mother's jewellery, his first instalment.

'So, let me get this straight you ordered a hit on your own elders and Raghu managed to do all of this, he bought a gun, a knife, and some gloves but what for money', stating the facts while roaming around Ajay.

'He said he would also look for something valuable in the house, if he finds it he would keep it', said Arun.

Kid, hey kid look at me, you know murder is murder right, I wish I could save you, believe me, I can understand your pain and embarrassment but it's not in my hands now the judge will decide what will happen. You are just 19 you could have a bright future for yourself but now it is going to be very tough for you. You said you were doing this for your parents; now think about it, how they would feel when they think about you. That their kid is a murderer. Said Ajay.

'That's enough Ajay! Let's go to the station and arrest Raghu and his friend who has these contacts for the conspiracy of murder', ordering Officer Yashwant.

End Scene:

Constable Rathi caught Raghu and after three blows on his leg with a police wooden baton, he confessed to the killings of Mr and Mrs Kumar.

5

The Village

Kali Sitholey Rawat

An abandoned village, Rajasthan June 17th, 2001.

The jeep stuttered to a halt and died a spluttering, wheezing death in the middle of the dusty road. 'Engine trouble Madam!' announced my driver rather gleefully. 'Great, just great!' I muttered as I jumped out of the jeep to stretch my legs. This research trip to long abandoned villages in Rajasthan was turning out to be more of an exercise in developing patience than anything else.

'Ok' I told him. 'I'll walk around till you fix it.' I grabbed my water bottle and scarf and set out on foot to explore the derelict ruins that were once an ancient but glorious and prosperous agricultural town. I won't lie; I was nervous. A single woman, travelling to remote and "barely civilized" areas in Rajasthan evoked strong reactions from friends and family alike. Ranging from "it's just not safe", to "what exactly are you looking for?" The comments if anything, made me even more pigheadedly determined to strike out on my own. The only comment which stuck with me was, 'You are aware that these places are haunted, right?' from my brutally honest friend, D.

But even that did not deter me. I was excited as I entered the huge gate made of crumbling bricks which marked the entrance to the village. It was desolate, eerie and beautiful. Little whirlpools of dust swirled under my feet as I walked the narrow crisscrossing lanes. Most houses were in a state of terrible disrepair, roofless - with windows like black eyes staring back at me, literally daring me to enter. I didn't; it was approaching dusk, and the place was making me nervous.

Deciding to return to the car, I began to retrace my steps back to the entrance but lost track of the way out! I went back to the lanes I had come from, noting with mounting relief familiar structures and features on houses that I had passed on my way in. But when I reached the end of the lane which should have taken me to the entrance gate, I found that it further bifurcated into two other lanes! 'Damn it!' I cursed and pulled out my phone to see if I could call the driver for help, but there was no service. 'Of course!' I muttered to myself.

The light was fading fast, and with it, my courage. The temperature was dropping quickly as well, and I thanked my lucky stars that I had brought my scarf along, for whatever little protection it offered me. My water bottle was almost half empty now, I realized I would need a refill soon. I decided to explore the leftmost lane first and picked up a handful of pebbles, which I placed at fixed intervals of 5 feet along the road so as to mark my progress. I walked quite a distance, but the road wound round and round the village till I ended up exactly where I had started! Extremely frustrated I looked to see whether the stones I had placed were still there and sure enough, there they were; shiny little pebbles which confounded me more than anything else.

'Ok then' I thought 'let's try the lane to the right' I set off, winding my scarf tightly about me. (To my great irritation, the silky fabric would keep slipping off, no matter how tightly I knotted it.) It was very dark now, and I was close to a full-blown panic attack. Taking deep breaths, I plunged on, using the torch function on my Nokia cell phone to illuminate the narrow and dusty path. I tripped and fell on the jagged stones in my way, which ripped through my jeans and sliced open my knee.

Whimpering, I got up mentally debating whether to use the remaining water in my bottle to clean the wound when I heard the unmistakable sound of children giggling at my predicament. 'Oh

Thank God!' I cried out. 'Please help me, I am lost' I turned around to say to the kids I heard behind me. Only, there was nobody there.

I RAN.

Abandoning all sense of direction and caution to the wind, I ran as fast as I could, on any path that opened up in my way. I kept straining to hear the sounds of feet running behind me, but didn't hear anything, and winded, slumped against the wall of a relatively well-maintained house which I had never noticed before.

Shining my phone light on it, I saw that it had some lovely geometric motifs painted on its walls, and it was larger and comparatively better preserved than any of the structures around it. I entered the doorway to a large courtyard which led to a series of doors flanking it on three sides. 'This must have been the home of someone important' I thought to myself, and I approached the door.

I was frightened but also realized that I would have to spend the night in this abandoned village, as there was no hope of my exiting this place in pitch dark. I just prayed that the driver would wait for me, or better yet come looking for me, though the way he had reacted when I asked him to drive me here- 'Why go there, Madam? Very bad place' made me doubt it.

I was still frightened of the children's voices I had heard (or imagined?) and decided to see if I could pass the night in one of the rooms. I walked into the first room to a horrible acrid stench. It was so foul that I ran out gasping for breath, and decided to try my luck in the next room. However, that room also had the same foul air. Shining my light around the room, I saw why: the ceiling was covered with bats. Shuddering, I plunged through the dark depths hoping to find an inner room which would serve my purpose of a bedroom for a night. There was a small doorway which looked to be opening up into a small antechamber but when I entered it, I found it was a longish corridor. Walking along the length of the corridor, I stumbled once more, this time dropping my phone and losing my only source of light in the bargain. Cursing my clumsiness, I realized the phone's torch had broken and I was now in pitch-black darkness.

It wasn't the darkness that scared me; it was the sound of children giggling again, this time right over my shoulder. I screamed out of fear, only to have my scream, the same tone, the same volume and exactly the same pitch shouted right back at me, shouted in many different voices in my ear, their cold breaths on my neck making me shiver uncontrollably. Stumbling to my feet, I ran down the corridor, this time the giggling voices with no faces to them following right behind me. I was sobbing while I ran, but the voices, cruel in the typical way children can be; laughed even louder at my obvious terror, all the while chasing me, chasing me.

I lost track of how long or how far I ran, all I noted was that the corridor was progressively sloping downwards, sometimes at angles so steep that my feet slipped on the smooth stone surface, much to the delight of my faceless tormentors. Exhausted, I reached a place in my mind where I began to contemplate turning back around and running right at the voices for lack of any other options when I saw a series of steps cut into the left of the corridor. I dashed onto them and quickly descended into some sort of subterranean chamber. The quality of air changed here, it was damp and dank- thick.

I reached the bottom of the steps to discover that they led to a huge pond of water. It was a stepwell! Built centuries ago to collect rainwater and to provide rest and refuge to tired travellers and locals, step-wells were literally deep wells cut into the ground, accessed by a series of steps. This particular one must have served the village I had walked through, and I must have run through a corridor which leads directly from the village to the stepwell.

This particular stepwell was very, very deep. Looking up, I saw a distant sliver of light through its cracked roof and realized that night had passed, and it was early morning. I wept with relief and after making sure that there was nobody following me, sat down on the steps next to the brackish water which seemed to be covered with a thick layer of green algae. 'I'll just catch my breath and then climb the steps to the top' I thought to myself and bent to check my cell phone.

I never felt the hand that pushed me in, only heard the cruel laughter of the children as I flailed in the slimy water to stay afloat. There must have been weeds in its depths, for something grabbed my feet and prevented me from coming to the surface of the water. That's the last thing I remember.

I came to the steps of the well; I don't remember how I got there, or who saved me. All I could hear is the children's voices, angry now, sibilant petulant vexed voices, no doubt angry over my making it out in one piece. This time I didn't wait, I fled back up the stairs, through the corridor and into the room through which I had entered this cursed passage. I ran out into the open streets to a starry, open sky and laughed a manic laugh, free at last from that hell hole. I felt the earth spin and fall to a heap on the ground.

I don't know how long I was unconscious but when I came to, the sun was blazing brightly in the sky. A group of Asian tourists was chattering excitedly and taking pictures of the motifs painted on the walls of the large house. 'Help me!' I croaked, reaching out to the chubby man next to me. He was oblivious, staring intently at the intricate patterns. But even though I was only three feet away from him, he ignored me. I tried to find my feet but had lost the strength to walk, so I dragged myself to the lady he was standing next to. I tried to grab her leg- 'please!' I managed. She turned around with a surprised expression but appeared not to notice me. I was shocked at the callousness of these people! Mustering up every bit of strength I had left, I screamed at the top of my voice 'HELP!' There was no response. I couldn't understand it!

Disheartened, I slumped back against the wall. I decided to pick up pebbles and throw them at the tourists to attract their attention and was scrabbling about looking for some when I saw the children who tormented me standing right in front of me. 'It's no use! They laughed cruelly at me.

I whipped around to gauge the reaction of the Asian group to see such a large group of children materialize literally out of thin air. But there was none at all. The group was oblivious to them, to us, to me.

'Don't you understand?' they sang in a horrible macabre song as they circled me, holding hands while they skipped. 'Am I dead?' I wailed 'Oh God! Am I dead?' I begged them for an answer.

They didn't answer, of course, the nasty, cruel children that they were.

6

A Doctor's Verdict

Reggie Menacherry

The End:

Sealed inside a hotel room, Dr Praneet Kumar was calmly sitting on a recognizable chair with a blunt blade pressed on the nerves of his own wrist. Dr Praneet knew this was the same room where even he committed suicide. 'I can feel his presence.' He even read the name carved inside the wooden study table in the hotel room. They say memories erupt in front of you when your life approaches, "the end." The reels of Dr Praneet Kumar's life exploded in his memories.

The Crime:

A few months back, during a routine check-up day, Dr Kumar got a frantic call to race into the operation theatre on an ordinary check-up day. He was wrestling to make his way through a stubborn screaming group of villagers outside. Suddenly a cop grabbed his wrist and pulled him out towards the operation theatre door. A young man in a critical situation was profusely bleeding, lying half-dead on the operation table, and seemed to have been thrashed multiple times with stones and bamboo. After a 6-hour life battling operation, Dr Kumar found the villagers had apprehended this man whose life he saved 10mins back while attempting to escape the crime scene after raping and brutally stabbing a girl. While, In the above operation room, the same girl died on an operation table.

The Pressure:

Media circus muddled with protestors was now outside the hospital more because the murderer was the son of a powerful MLA. Even Dr Kumar was unsettled by the media's heckling and nuisance behaviour. He suspended his social media accounts to refrain from the trolls for saving a murderer's life. In 24 hours, his life was in complete chaos and unwanted limelight. Three days later, Dr Kumar faces the victim's mother by informing her, of her husband's death on his operation table. Dr Kumar was devasted by witnessing two deaths from the same family in his hospital. The latest news about the victims' father being killed by the murderer's family under the cover-up of a road accident was ignited like wildfire. His hatred amplified day by day during every medical consultation with the murderer. This murderer will never step inside a prison because the case will be withdrawn back by the victim's mother. The MLA threatened her that her younger daughter's life would be in danger. During one of his consultations, Dr Kumar regarded these rumours in an intelligent interrogation manner where he imperilled the murderer's egoistic manhood. The murderer proudly alleged his ability to play with people's lives and how he controls the very fate of the case from the hospital bed. His smirking face with no remorse set anger and rage anchored in Dr Kumar's heart. More than anger, a pang of guilt grew in his heart for saving this devil's life. A psychotic man will haunt women on the streets because of him. Each time he saw his mother and sister returning home from work late evenings, his conscience got dragged into the same guilt trip. Those horrific post-mortem scenes and the murderers smirking faces haunted him every minute.

The Friend:

He would sneak to repose in the medical college's library within his hospital compound. One night he was unwinding in the library all alone. A friendly voice at 3:00 A.M. stirred his sleepy eyes with transient shock. 'Aha! Our infamous Dr is hibernating here.' A fine young physician in his mid-20s now sat across from him; Dr Yash Upadhyay was his self-introduction. Even though Dr Kumar pestered with his heckling statement, he couldn't neglect his smooth composure and eye-catching persona. After a few minutes of chattering about the media circus and online bullying, Dr Kumar vented his frustration about the entire diabolical.

The Guilt:

'You Dumbass!' Dr Upadhyay interrupted his raving rant, 'I would have never saved the life of that evil lunatic.' Dr Kumar's few seconds of sarcastic laughter turned into jaw-dropping disarray. 'Fuck the Hippocratic oath. There are lunatics and criminals like him on the streets. They are raping women, killing innocent people for mere entertainment, and flaunting their muscle power. Are we supposed to vent our frustration on our family, Facebook, or Twitter? When that guy walks out and picks his next victim, that bloodstain will be on your conscience, Dr Kumar.' His every single word sliced through Dr Kumar's cerebra deeper than a scalpel. Dr Kumar could only utter one word to break his silence 'But!'. Dr Upadhyay's charisma and powerful tone could make anyone listen to him. 'Shut up, Shut up! You crazy fucker!', Dr Kumar screamed while attempting to flee from the library, covering his ears. Dr Upadhyay ran behind Dr Kumar, caught his collar, and slammed his back on the door of the old shelf. 'You are a fucking coward. One day when you get summoned to identify the mutilated body of your sister or the day she dies in front of you from a sexual assault, possibly from that guy itself. It's only from that day your remorseful life will begin. You rich doctors will probably send your loved ones to safe urban cities away from these villages or other countries. But what about...' In a wave of rage, Dr Kumar slapped him, pushed him with force, and faded into the hostel corridor.

The Avenge:

Dr Upadhyay's words were like an inferno burning his brains, flaming every nerve of conscience and every word of the Hippocratic oath into ashes. For days without proper sleep, he was trapped in fear of unconsciously imagining his own sister's body lying in front of him on the operation table screaming, only one word, "Avenge." Dr Kumar's repeated request to transfer the criminal's case to another doctor got rejected. Meanwhile, during his multiple consultations, his criminal patient never showed any guilt. His pride in killing people in broad daylight and getting away with it with no legal ramifications was getting more significant. Dr Kumar got convinced that this criminal was a lunatic, waiting for his next prey. His soul was dark and deliciously feeding on weak people.

The Hero:

Two days later, breaking news flashed across all screens throughout the country regarding the demise of the criminal due to a sudden cardiac arrest. Social media went bizarre in a victory uproar, claiming it to be God's verdict. Some people argued political vendetta, while some claimed this was an inside act by law and order. Nonetheless, Dr Kumar felt relaxed for a moment; the maiming from trolls and media pressure was over. Though he laughed at some lunatics claiming he was the one who delivered the justice. Soon, he never got a peaceful sleep hereafter; there was a mammoth guilt trip making his hands tremble even in the operation theatre. He was no more the man he knew he was.

The Secret:

A few months later, while Dr Kumar was scrolling through a few books for his research, he came across one familiar-looking book. He quickly remembered that Dr Upadhyay was holding a similar one that night. He casually flipped through the pages to find an envelope with an enclosed letter addressed: 'One who finds may choose to pursue this story or burn this letter. A confession of life and love.' He leapt to the corner of the room under a study lamp and began reading.

The Story:

The letter elegantly expresses a young doctor falling in love with a beautiful girl from the village. It was love at first sight for him, but more of one-sided love. After a few weeks, he got the news about her wedding in the same village. A month later, the same girl visited him for a consultation. This beautiful girl became his regular visitor under some questionable circumstances. She would sometimes come to him with a black eye, a sprained leg, a fractured hand, and all that within just a month. She averted by giving him weird reasons until the day she came to him with a busted head. Taking him into confidence, she did confess to domestic abuse by her husband. Discreetly, he complained about the incident to the cops, who never took the complaint seriously, claiming the girl would not support him and would refuse to register a case. In the village, this was the same sad story for many women.

The Confession:

Throughout the consultations, both developed a bond of friendship that steadily blossomed into a doctor's fantasy love. One day, he had to save her life from a snake bite while learning the snake in her room was the act of her husband. For Dr Yash Upadhyay, this was the last straw drawn. One afternoon, her husband was bought to his dispensary in a passed-out condition after overdosing from country-made alcohol. The doctor did not try to save his life inside that small emergency room, where they both were alone. He eventually passed away in a few hours.

A grieving wife slowly submitted to being a lover on his supporting shoulders. "Justice was served and should be served, Fuck the Hippocratic Oath. For Love and Justice.", signing off Dr Yash Upadhyay.

The Revenge:

'You! killer asshole! You put my life through hell, you sick! And soon after killing someone, you want to live a happy married life.' Dr Kumar yelled and stormed to the librarian's desk, demanding the contact details of Dr Yash Upadhyay. From the College Dean's register, he did find his residential address.

It was midnight, and like a madman, Dr Kumar started screaming and banging on the door challenging him to come out, confront, or face the law. An old man in his late sixties opened the door with a rifle, screaming, 'You drunkard stay off from my property, or I will shoot.' Dr Kumar stumbled behind, reckoning that he must have got the wrong address. 'I'm sorry for the trouble. I was desperate to hand over a letter to a Dr Yash Upadhyay.' The Old Man stopped and informed him that he was the father of Yash Upadhyay.

Dr Kumar commands the Old Man to demand his son's presence immediately. Yash's father stretched his hand ahead and asked to hand him over the letter. Dr Kumar's refusal forced Yash's father to point the rifle at Kumar's forehead, screaming at him, 'Hand it over to me.' Dr Kumar hands the envelope with a trembling voice to Yash's Father, 'Please! I must speak to Yash and need answers from him. It's regarding the letter.' 'Did you know if Yash is in love with someone woman from the village?' Dr Kumar asked. With a concerned and questionable voice, Yash's father replied, 'Yes! I did know about that...' Dr Kumar knelt, folding his hands and tears in his eyes, begging him to inform him about his son's whereabouts. The Old Man slams the gate close, unsure of the doctor's intentions. After an hour, Yash's father storms out of his house, and upon seeing Kumar standing outside the gate, he grabs his collar in anger and questions him, 'What kind of sick joke is this? Why are you trying to tarnish my son?' Dr Kumar tries to calm down Yash's father and informs him how this letter came into his possession. 'And If this is true, I'm sorry you can't meet Yash; he passed away,' replied his dad in a grieving tone.

Dr Kumar collapses on his knee, screeching and uprooting the grass from the roadside. Yash's Father held him in his hands and tried to reason his suicidal death. Dr Kumar wanted to speak to the girl and find out if she knew anything more about his story. Yash's father claimed he did try many times to talk to her, but all in vain. But this time, she might converse if they tell her that they know about their story.

More Secrets:

The morning of watching Yash's father at her doorstep, her anger erupted like a volcano. Dr Kumar blatantly screamed, 'We know! We Know Yash killed your late husband'. Hearing these words, 'She hugged Yash's father, 'I'm sorry! and it's because of me, you lost your son.' Yash's father and Dr Kumar were confused and perplexed at her response. After 15 mins of consoling her, she started narrating the rest of the story; from where Yash's letter ends.

One day, Yash confessed to her how he killed her late husband. And what he did to protect her life and give her life a second chance. She slapped him multiple times, calling him a "Murderer" and yelling at him how she could not spend the rest of her life with him. 'Few days after our breakup, we lost Yash forever. I never wanted this to happen.'

Yash's father and Dr Kumar did not speak to each other the entire journey back home. At Yash's father's request, Dr Kumar agreed to have a cup of tea at his house. Dr Kumar closely approached Yash's photo frame hanging on the wall. He read, "My Loving Son, A Doctor who saved lives, 1975–2002." Surprised, he smiled back at Yash's father, 'Uncle, you probably need to get your eyes checked up. You have printed 2002.' The old man reached close to the photo frame cleaning his spectacles, 'No! Dr Kumar, 2002 it is.'

The Beginning of the End:

Dropping the teacup, and shoving Yash's father away, he flew from the scene, driving back to the college library. He was scared and clueless;

the thin line of hope he had been alive for a few months started fading away. His reality of killing a criminal was no more real to him. While driving his car, he couldn't believe how he let himself kill someone. With his heart pounding in disbelief and shock, Dr Kumar scuffled for the library card of the same book submitted by Yash. The book return date signed by Yash was "19th September 2002."

Walking back to his room, Dr Kumar looked at every hanging calendar in the hallway, reading today's date, 19th September 2006.

Meanwhile, in a puzzled state of mind, the librarian flipped through the pages of the research book Dr Kumar was questioning, "The Mystery of Psychosis."

7

The Chase

Aanika Gajendragad

'Good job, Dhruth!' His coach told him as Dhruth felt him patting his back. 'If you practice a little more, I'm sure you'll come first in the competition. You're already the best in the district.'

He crossed the road carefully, gripping his white cane. He was on his way to his boarding school from his favourite cafe. He felt exhausted after a good four hours of running. He loved to run when he was a child. The fact that he was blind didn't stop him. He was practising for his state-level sprint competition. Entering his room to rest, he immediately drifted off to deep sleep.

Suddenly he woke to loud sirens inside the building. He could hear people outside shouting, 'Fire emergency! Evacuate the building!' He got up and started running towards the stairs to leave the building and saw people pacing side to side. After a lot of getting pushed around in between people, he finally got to take a good look at the building. He watched in fear as the fire engulfed the building, and firemen rushed around, trying to diffuse the fire. He noticed a blind person on the roads, whom he guessed to be from the boarding school, struggling to cross it. Dhruth picked his stick up and guided him to the other side, like any person helping a blind man. It was at that time that he noticed he could see. That left the lad wondering how it was possible. He felt a tap on his back and turned to see a man in beach shorts and a loose white t-shirt. He was pleasantly surprised at his choice of clothing on a weekday. The man looked so relaxed, no one could tell he was standing in front of a building on fire. His white beard cascaded down his chest, slightly curled at the end. He wore a red cap on his head, sea-blue eyes shining from under his spectacles. 'Care to have pizza with me?' He asked, staring into his eyes. He was so manipulative that Dhruth couldn't say no. Plus when an elderly was treating a younger one, it usually meant they would pay. Who would reject free pizza? He nodded and followed the man as if in trance. Dhruth looked at the building, which was now black of smoke. The firemen continued to put out the fire.

The man walked to the cafe in front of the burning building. Dhruth quickly recognized it to be his favourite cafe. Now that he could see, he noticed no other cafe near the place. 'That's why the cafe was so crowded,' he thought to himself. Even though he ate before he slept, looking at the pizzas on the menu made his stomach grumble. Which was weird because he never ate much.

He was mesmerized by the view inside the cafe. Chains of fairy lights decorated the walls, and Polaroids of the customers were stuck in some places. A chandelier hung from the ceiling. The man sat on a chair, gesturing for Dhruth to sit in front of him. He played with the tiny plant in front of him. 'So, this is what a plant looks like,' he thought.

'The fire was all of a sudden, do you know why that happened?' The man asked. Before Dhruth could speak, the man continued, 'You had a good sleep?' Dhruth nodded, asking him the same question. 'Ah, yes. I even got a dream that felt so real. I think I was talking in my sleep too.' The man laughed, even his laugh felt pleasing to Dhruth. 'Dreams are much more real than the real world, aren't they?' He spoke again. Dhruth simply nodded again. 'My dream ended abruptly. I might just go and continue it after everything settles,' the man said.

'How can you do that?' Dhruth seemed intrigued. The man let out a small chuckle again. 'I just remember what happened the last in my dream before going to sleep. Then I let my mind do the rest.' Suddenly Dhruth felt someone hit his head from behind. Before he could see who it is, he collapsed on the ground.

He groaned and massaged his head. He couldn't see anything. By the smell and sounds coming from outside, he recognized it to be his dorm room. 'So, it was all a dream,' he muttered to himself. 'I wanted that pizza though.' He tutted and stood up. He found it strange how he could see in his dream and not in reality. He wondered if he had got that kind of dream because of his fear of fire. It was because of fire that he lost his sight, after all. When he was just a toddler. He wondered if the man in beach shorts did something to him to get his sight back in the dream. You couldn't blame him for thinking that way, anyone would get attracted to the man. Like how people agree with everything their favourite idol says, or like the man was a mind controller.

He couldn't stop thinking about his dream the whole day, even when he practised running. The coach even scolded him for not concentrating. But Dhruth was too occupied in his thoughts. He wanted to have a dream where he can see again. He wanted to meet the eerie yet peaceful man again. He thought about everything they spoke about, trying to remember every detail. That's when he remembered what the man had talked about sleeping again and getting the same dream. 'I must try it,' he muttered to himself. 'Let me grab some pizza before I go, the pizza in my dream has caused me to crave it.' He went to the cafe again. The owners were familiar with him by this time, he visited very often. 'Can I have a Margherita, please?' He heard a voice say. The voice aroused Dhruth. He never thought he would be attracted to someone by their voice. Disregarding the thought, he satisfied himself by eating and walking to his room. After a lot of turning around on his bed, he finally fell asleep. He didn't forget to remember what had happened in his previous dream before going to sleep. He just thought of the strange dude.

He was in the same cafe as before, just the man wasn't in front of him. He saw the fire trucks parked in front of the cafe and decided to get a glimpse of his now-burnt boarding school of his. 'Quite an obnoxious sight, eh?' He heard someone say. A boy around his age stood next to him. Dhruth was sure he had heard the voice before; he just couldn't recognize the owner. The boy had sea-blue eyes that Dhruth swore he had seen before. 'Yeah,' he replied softly. 'You live there, don't you?' The boy asked him. Dhruth nodded.

'I do too. Atharv. Nice to meet you,' he said, extending his hand for a shake. Dhruth took it and smiled at him. 'I'm Dhruth. Where-' he got interrupted by a girl crying for help.

'Why is everyone's voice sounding similar to mine?' He sighed.

'Excuse me please,' Dhruth said to Atharv as he walked over and asked what the matter was. 'My dog- he's still in the building! He-' Dhruth started walking towards the building without letting her continue. He knew the building even with his eyes closed. He heard yelps coming from a room- his room. He saw the dog stuck between his desks when he ran to his room. Slowly picking the dog up, Dhruth examined the injury on its leg, quickly wrapping a piece of cloth around it.

'Thank you so much!' The girl said when he finally came down and handed the dog to her. She had hazel eyes that went perfectly with her cinnamon-brown hair. Dhruth couldn't get his eyes off her. Then he remembered where he had heard the voice- it was at the cafe, the same voice that had attracted him. 'My poor dog hurt his leg,' she said softly to herself as she walked away. Dhruth wondered why there was a dog in a boarding school. He watched as the girl's figure disappeared.

To his surprise, the girl soon returned and gave him a pile of money as a gratitude gift. 'It's the least I can do, please take it.'

'I couldn't let a dog alone, it's the least I could do, don't worry.' He replied.

'I still need to repay you somehow, tell me how I can.'

'I don't want anything.' Dhruth smiled.

'Please,' she begged.

'What's your name?' He asked her.

'Idika.'

'Hi Idika, I'm Dhruth. Would you like to have pizza with me?' Dhruth asked without thinking. For some reason, he was getting hungrier every hour.

'Sure,' she gave him a genuine smile before leading the way.

'One Margherita, please,' she said to the waiter. 'What would you-what's so funny?' She asked when she saw Dhruth giggling to himself. 'Nothing,' he answered with a straight face, laughing at her love for Margheritas. She frowned at him. 'I would like to have a veggie pizza, please,' he said to the waiter who nodded and walked away.

'I heard you here yesterday,' he told her.

'Really? Only heard?' She tilted her head.

'Um, well, yeah.' He didn't want to tell her he was blind. He felt she would walk away from him. 'How didn't I notice you?' She asked. He shrugged, keeping his head low.

'Oh, I have a sprint competition next week, it would be great to have you there.' He lit up every time he spoke about running.

'You're in the competition? Oh my god, I love watching those!' She exclaimed, which excited Dhruth more. They continued to speak for a while until Idika's parents called and she had to go. 'I'll be there cheering for you next week!' She chirped and waved at him after exchanging numbers. She thanked him again for saving her dog, whose name was apparently Oscar. She said she kept the name so because if she wasn't successful in the future and didn't get an Oscar award, she could still say she has Oscar. He smiled to himself and got up to walk out too until he felt himself being shaken continuously. He shut his eyes.

When he opened them, he could see "nothing." 'Dhruth!' His friend shouted. He realized he was in his dorm room. He was so into his dream that he forgot it was one. He wondered if Idika would still come to the competition. “No, it was just a dream,” he reminded himself, erasing his thoughts. It made him disappointed. He would still search for her in the field on the day. “But the dream was just my imagination, how do I know if she looks the same?” He sighed. Because of the voice he had heard first in the cafe, his evil mind had created an image and name for the voice. Now he couldn’t get her face out of his mind. He cursed at his mind repeatedly.

‘Finally, you’re awake!’ His friend said. Dhruth felt him hold a sound horn and raised an eyebrow. ‘I tried to wake you up a lot. You were asleep for two days. I was genuinely concerned. Even coach tried to wake you up and asked me to check on you multiple times,’ he said to Dhruth.

‘That would’ve been embarrassing,’ Dhruth said to them, knowing his coach didn’t care for them until they were running well and making him proud. He never cared if they overslept.

‘It was,’ his friend chuckled. ‘Come on now, Coach would kill me if he knew you’re awake without going for practice.’ Dhruth nodded and got out of bed.

‘Dude, you were sleeping like the guy in Ramayana. Ravana’s brother.’ His friend nudged him as they walked to the ground.

‘Kumbhkaran?’ Dhruth chuckled.

‘Yeah, him.’ The mystery of his dreams was left unsolved, so he decided to try again that night.

8

Immortal

Nilkesh Sonawane

It was very late at night; I was walking home. The street was empty. It was so quiet. The only sound I could hear was my own steps. It was a straight road, and there was no footpath, so I was walking on the road. And suddenly I saw a car coming from a distance at a normal speed. As it was about to cross me, suddenly, out of nowhere a dog jumped in front of the car, barking very loudly. The driver lost his control and the car turned towards me, and within a second, it hit me! I was thrown away from the street; before losing consciousness.

I had no idea for how long I was unconscious. When I woke up, someone was standing in front of me. I assumed he must be the driver. I touched my head, but it was fine. There was no blood, no bruises. I was completely okay. The car crashed. The driver bent over to me, and he looked into my eyes.

'You are immortal now' he said.

'What does that supposed to mean!' I exclaimed.

'Listen to me carefully, don't panic.' He said, 'I was Immortal, I have lived for two hundred years, I got this gift from someone. But only later on I learned, being immortal is a curse rather than a gift.' His face was all serious, but there was also some grief on his face, 'When everyone you know dies one by one, there comes a time when there is nobody known to you in this whole world. But, if you want to end your life, you can, by intentionally trying to kill yourself, you will die. But apart from that, nothing can kill you, NOTHING! And if you want to give this Immortality to someone else, you can. You just have to kill them!' he said, very surely.

'What the hell is this? Is this some kind of prank!?' I stood up.

'No, my friend, it's not a prank, I was thinking for many years, that whom should I give this Immortality, But I gave it to you tonight, accidentally. I hit you with the car, which means I killed you. You died, and you became immortal. See, there is not a single scar on your body! You are immortal.' He had a weirdly convincing confidence on his face.

I stared at him for a few seconds, it was so unbelievable. But, by the look on his face, anybody could have said, it was real.

'I have no way to believe you.' I said quietly.

'Yes, you don't, but you have to' he said with the same look.

I turned and picked up my bag and started walking back.

'Remember one thing' he yelled, 'If you gave someone your Immortality, you will become Mortal.'

I nod at him and kept walking. I didn't say anything. I looked back over my shoulders once, he was still there, looking at me.

When I reached home, I looked out my window more than 3 times. I wanted to speak to Veena, but she was sleeping & I didn't want to wake her up. I sat next to her. I was thinking about this incident for almost an hour. Was that real? Was that some kind of prank? But there was nobody except us. So what is this? What if he was telling the truth? Was he immortal? Was he hundred years old? Am I really immortal now? But how can I know it? He said only I can kill myself, which means, I cannot try it myself, someone else has to do that for me. But why would someone kill me, even if I asked for it? There was literally no way for me to check if that was true.

Several months passed by. It was Tuesday morning. I was sleeping on my bed and then I woke up. The sun was up. It was late in the morning. There was no noise coming from the kitchen. I wondered if Veena was up yet. I got up. Veena was still sleeping, beside me. The alarm didn't ring? I shook her. But she wasn't responding. I shook her again, but there was no response. I did it again and again. I was scared, I checked her pulse, I checked her breath, and she was breathing. It calmed me a little. I called an ambulance. After 15 minutes of long waiting, the ambulance arrived. When I heard the ambulance siren, my skin crawled. I realized, "When the ambulance passes you on the road, it doesn't make you feel anything, but when that siren is for someone, you love, it hits you hard".

They took her to the hospital, doctors started working immediately. There were several tests they were performing. She was still unconscious. A few hours went by. I saw from the small window, she was awake, shocked to find herself in the hospital. The nurse was filling her in, I wanted to talk to her. But the doctor called me. I went in.

'What is it doc?' I asked. I sat on a chair next to him.

'Listen to me carefully, don't panic' the doctor said as he leaned over his chair.

'We did some tests on Veena, and we have found that she has a brain tumour.' The doctor took a pause after that sentence, to see my reaction. I was numb. He continued, 'Compared to other cases, this one is pretty big.'

'bu..' I stuttered. 'but, it is curable, right?

'It is a grade four tumour; it cannot be treated. We can use chemo to slow down its growth, but it's not curable.' Doctor said.

I was lost. I couldn't bare it. I couldn't digest the fact that my beloved wife was going to die.

'How much time has she got?' I asked, hoping for a few years.

'Maximum two or three months.' The doctor said with a sad face, 'And with the help of chemo, we may stretch it more. But the next few months are going to be tough. Especially for you. Veena would be no longer the person you used to know. Her personality, her behaviour will change, she will act strange, you have to get yourself ready for what's coming.'

I kept looking at the doctor. I couldn't even cry, I tried, but couldn't. They discharged her after a few days. I brought her home. Those days were bad, we didn't even talk to each other for some days.

Several days went by, I started taking care of her. I left my job. I had plenty of savings. I used to make breakfast, lunch and dinner for her. I used to bathe her and do everything; everything that I could.

One day, when I put her to sleep and sat before her. I tried imagining my life after her death. And I couldn't even think of it. It was unimaginable. Then it came to my mind. Immortal! I had almost forgotten that incident. I thought, 'If it's true, it'll be like letting my wife die when I have a chance to save her. But if it's true, I will have to kill my wife. And if it's not true, I will be killing my wife before the tumour kills her!'

I sat there. Thinking, 'the tumour is going to kill Veena anyway. And even if I decided to kill Veena, how will I kill her? With a knife? By slicing her throat? Or by strangling her? But strangling her how? With a rope or with my bare hands!? She will scream, it will be unbelievable for her to watch her husband strangling her to death. What if the police caught me? No! they won't, she is not actually dying, and there won't be any murder. But what about Veena? Should I talk to her about it? No, she won't believe me! What if I killed her in her sleep? She will be immortal even before waking up. But, if I succeed, will she be, okay? Can immortality cure her tumour? Should I ask the doctors about it? of course not! IDIOT!' I cursed and hit my forehead. All these thoughts were crushing my mind. I didn't know if I was really immortal or not, what if that guy was a psychopath? An exploiter! Or maybe he was, he was speaking the truth.

The next morning when I woke up, I googled, 'easy ways to die', but google gave me the results for helplines; it thought I was committing suicide. Then I tried differently. I typed, "Easy ways to kill someone," but again he showed me the same results. Useless!

Veena began to act strangely! She began saying things she would never say. She lost her interest in everything. After a month, she never left the room. She used to sleep all day and nothing else.

The hospital called me. Her surgery date was closed. There was no guarantee of that operation, a 50-50 chance.

So, I made my decision. I will make her immortal, right before the operation. My plan also had a 50-50 chance, either this thing could be true or fake! But I am willing to take the chance. Because if I didn't do anything, and something happened to her during the operation. I couldn't forgive myself.

I planned everything, I will give her poison right before the operation, so, even if it didn't work, the blame will go on the doctors. The operation was supposed to be done in two weeks. I decided to spend every minute with Veena before the surgery, And I did, the next few days I sat next to her, holding her hand, she knew her death was near. We cried, and we laughed. She empathized,

'I will be waiting for you at the other end' she said.

'I promise you, it's me, who will be waiting. You are going to live a very long life.' I cried.

Finally, the day came. She was moved to the ICU. They were going to shift her to the operation centre within 1 hour. She was given some steroids, she was asleep. I had bought the poison from my friend's medical store. I had it all prepared. I checked the room and the corridor, to make sure no one is coming. I filled up the injection with the poison. I looked at Veena, even in sleep, she was looking so beautiful. I grabbed her hand. The only thought coming to my mind was, right or wrong. This either goes right or wrong. But what if I happen to be the reason for her death? No! No! No! I don't have time for it right now, I have to do it! I pulled out the injection, and started injecting it in her vein. I was shaking. The thought of it was killing me.

Suddenly, I heard the nurse coming, I immediately pulled out the injection and hide it in my pocket. I was also a bit scared that she might have seen me. She gave me a prescription and told me to bring those medicines. I took the list and went outside. I had only 45 minutes left. I had to hurry up. The medical was on the other side of the highway. I rushed to the medical, bought the medicine, and was heading back to the hospital.

While crossing the street, it crossed my mind again!

Did I save her? How will I know? I guess she will just wake, just like I did? But will she? What if she dies? What if all this was a joke?! What if he was lying? Was I really saved from that car accident? Did the accident really killed me? Was I really dead? Or just unconscious?! I don't even know that man's name. As I was thinking about it, out of nowhere one car came running, out of control. Some people were screaming "Break fail! Break fail!" the car turned towards me! Before I could move from there, I was thrown in the air. The car hit me with full force. When I fell to the ground, it was my head that touched the ground first. I lost consciousness. I remember thinking to myself, I must wake up! I have to see, did it work? Did I save veena? Or she died? Was this Immortality thing real? Or not? I have to hurry up! I have to wake up! But it never happened because I never woke up.

9

Doorstep

Vaishnavi Tawade

It's her birthday today, Maria my little child. Her silly laughter was the most precious thing in my life, little did I know this very silly laughter was the outbreak of her sneaking schizophrenia. Peter and I couldn't conceive a child for a good decade after our marriage, my parents had passed away when I was five and Peter's parents had died in a tragic car accident. We had no family, and the house was empty and gloomy like a haunted house, we both lived in that big mansion feeling extremely downhearted and dull, but then God answered all our prayers and blew our soul into our lifeless marriage. Maria's happiness became the purpose of our lives, we engaged her in all the extracurricular activities one could think of, and we wanted her to do it all.

But suddenly, all of it turned dismal. She was 18 when we started hearing screeching sounds from her room at night, we thought it was a cat and ignored it. She started eating her lunch and dinner in her room and spoke to herself, but we thought she was just entertaining herself; Maria was a goofy girl. Then things started getting intense, Maria walked out of the house at night and sat in our garden, digging a hole in the musty soil of a dead plant. She was laughing, crying and her eyes looked like the darkness in the sky had made a home in them. We started getting worried. Peter's age was ripe, I could see him leaving me slowly. Peter wasn't in the condition to walk to the bathroom, forget about finding answers to Maria's uncanny chaos. Peter passed away when Maria was 20. He wanted to see her daughter marry, and wear a beautiful white gown with pearls and roses adorning her beauty. Maria's marriage became my only resolve after Peter's death. Seeing her bizarre behaviour, I only thought that it came from the loneliness of being a single child and that getting her a partner would make it all right. I was wrong.

Maria ran away from the church before her marriage could proceed, and we kept searching for her everywhere. She returned four hours later; I could see her smiling and coming running towards me from afar. As Maria started getting closer, her now blurry face started getting clearer, she wasn't just smiling. Her white gown now dripping with blood, and our half-dead cat Lolo was in her hands. She came jumping towards me and hugged me tight and said, 'Mom! Look I gave him what he wanted mom, I gave him his gift mom, I know he will be my friend forever Mom'. I gripped her as tightly as I could, my heart shook, and all her would-be in-laws started whispering things I wasn't ready to hear. I missed Peter's presence strongly that day. All their jaws dropped, and they asked me to take her to an exorcist, but I knew my child was an angel. She was the purest and the most beautiful angel, but people's whispers started getting louder and so did the noises from Maria's room.

I didn't have a choice, I decided to take Maria to an exorcist, he confirmed that Maria had in fact been in the possession of a bloodthirsty demon and that her heinous acts were all a result of it. She was out of my control; I passed the grip to the exorcist and that's where I invited her misery. He came home at 7 every day, ripped apart her fingernails, made her bald and tied her to the bed saying that any dead cell on her body would make her more vulnerable to more demons. I could see my doll become hideous and awful. I couldn't look at her. Her eyes had become red from all the nights she didn't sleep and I couldn't understand a word of what she was uttering. I was scared.

One fine night I heard a loud banging noise from her room, I rang the line to the exorcist. He came within an hour with all his tools, Maria was out of control. My brittle old bones couldn't get a hold of her. The exorcist came and locked the door from the inside and told me to say a prayer. I couldn't mutter words, my heart started pounding in my chest and hearing her screams. Two hours later, the exorcist left and I slowly walked on my toes to her room. I opened the door and saw the sight of my peacefully sleeping fairy. I breathed with relief. I went back to my room and tried to sleep but I couldn't stop thinking about my little angel, and oh I forgot to give her a good night's kiss. It was chilly outside; I reached for my robe and went towards the stairs up her room. The door was open, I went closer, and Maria's bed was empty. She wasn't there. I searched for her around the house and told her not to hide. Told her that she's going to get married now so the childhood games and fun should be enough by now. I chuckled. She was hiding behind the stairs that lead towards the roof. She adorably called me 'Mumma... I'm here; Mumma, come find me.'

My weak knees struggled my way towards the stairs, and I saw her. She was near the edge of the roof running in circles. She wanted me to play with her, poor Maria. She was sick of the strict exorcist, I could understand. But he was her only saviour in my eyes. I got tired and told her to go to sleep and held hands while we walked down the stairs. She left the grip of my fingers suddenly and ran back to the roof saying she forgot something up there.

I followed her silly laughter and went up with her. When I reached up, Maria wasn't there. I thought she was hiding in the corner again. My sweet child always wants to play, so I kept searching for her. My old lost body was gasping for breath, but my eyes were wide open searching for my angel. I couldn't see her. My playful smile started to dissolve into a sharp heartache. I went towards the edge, my eyes slowly dropping down to a sight I wasn't ready to see. Maria had jumped down from the room in the garden to the same spot I saw her digging a hole which I repeatedly kept filling secretly, and my vision went blank. I had collapsed. I couldn't remember what happened after, but when I opened my eyes, Maria was sleeping in her casket.

Wearing a beautiful white gown and roses adorning her beauty. The exorcist said the demon had completed his motive and taken what he wanted, my beautiful angel. I knew my Maria wasn't the demon they said she was, I know she was my beautiful angel. I wondered whether the demons in Maria's life the resentful ghosts or the demons were in people's heads. I was her mother, I could see my child screaming for help, from the demons in her head. She wanted to be liberated. She found her release, an end to her torture.

I wish I would have extended my thoughts and heard her screams for help beyond people's whispers and frail beliefs. I wish I hadn't gone to an exorcist; I wish I hadn't invited her death to our doorstep. I wish...

10

Show Me What I Am

Aanika Gajendragad

Her head throbbed as she heard laughs around her. "Do our homework for us, or else," Saanvi warned. She fell to the ground as her enemy kicked her stomach and walked away. 'You better give it by the lunch break,' Rekha said in a sing-song voice, kicking her left shoulder. She felt the world go blurry as her eyes shut.

'Why are you late, Amaira?' Her math teacher asked when she entered the classroom.

'S-sorry sir, I had a stomach ache,' she stuttered.

'Lies. All lies. Stand near the board.' Amaira sighed and nodded. This was the fifth time in the week she got scolded for something she didn't do. She looked at Saanvi and Rekha, who tried to hold their laughter. 'What are you doing?' her teacher asked when she wasn't coming to the spot he asked her to.

'Oh, Amy, I'm really sorry for the trouble I caused you,' Saanvi whispered mockingly when she nears them. She threw her bag on her table- which was in front of Saanvi's and Rekha's, unfortunately- in frustration and cringe at the nickname. 'Behave, Amaira. Stand outside the class.' Her teacher ordered. At this point, she felt like crying. She could do nothing but listen to the snickers of the people she hated the most.

'Your principal called. He said you were rude to your Chemistry teacher. This is the second time this week, Amaira.' Her mother said when she came back from school. Amaira groaned, plopping on the couch. 'You were such a good child, what happened to you? We pay the fees for you to misbehave?'

'Mom, leave me alone, please,' Amaira replied.

'Am-' She let out a loud shout, interrupting her mother. She ran up the stairs and into her room, shutting the door with force. Leaving her mother in shock. She immediately burst into tears.

'Why does everyone treat me like that? Am I really that bad?' She spoke to herself, looking at the full-length mirror in front of her bed. 'I guess it's because I'm fat.' She held her waist. 'And ugly,' she added, wiping the tears from her cheeks. She thought she saw the reflection in the mirror blink when she was well aware she wasn't blinking. But she shrugged the thought and threw herself on the bed, kicking her legs in irritation. She eventually fell asleep.

Rubbing her puffy eyes, she found the time to be 7:30 in the evening. *'Start doing your math homework.'* She ignored the voice in her head. *'I said do your math homework.'*

'There's no use, I'm not going to school ever.' She fought back to her mind.

'Don't be ridiculous, go. Do it.' Regardless, Amaira took out her phone. Within seconds she put it back down and proceeded to walk to her table. 'What am I doing? I'm not going to attend school.' She thought to herself.

'You were being stubborn. I had to take control,' the mind said as if it had a voice of its own. She started doing her homework, and to her surprise, she knew every sum. But that couldn't be possible because she hated maths. And she was awful at it.

'Amaira,' her mother called out, knocking lightly on her door. 'Come for dinner, sweetheart. I'm sorry for shouting at you.'

Amaira's red face soon turned to a soft one as she replied, 'Yes mom, coming.' Her mother let out a gasp in shock.

'What the heck is wrong with me?' Amaira asked herself, hitting her head multiple times. *'Hitting it won't do anything. You'll only harm your head.'*

'Who are you? Get out! I don't want to eat!' She shouted to her head. Anyone near her would think she's a psychopath. She waited for her brain to respond like it did before but to no avail. 'Are you alive?' She asked it. No reply. 'Huh. Thank God.' She slept on the bed with a sigh.

'Amaira! Come on, the food will get cold!' Her mother said.

'I'm sick of my name being used so much now,' Amaira mumbled and shut her eyes, not caring to respond to her mother. She looked at her legs as they got out of bed and started walking towards the door. 'What? Stop, stop walking. Don't move,' she scolded her legs, hitting them to make them stop. The legs didn't listen and continued to walk as if they had a mind of their own. They walked until she forced them down. She only fell on the stairs with a loud thud, causing her mother to look up in alarm.

'Ugh, you're so stiff-necked.'

'So, you're not dead,' she said out loud.

'Who's not dead?' Her mother questioned. Amaira shook her head and climbed down like nothing happened when she was burning from embarrassment inside.

'You're doing something good for once.' The voice in her brain observed as she picked the piece of bottle gourd from the plate. Just hearing the voice made her change her decision. She immediately put the piece down, to which the voice spoke, 'You are such a birdbrain.'

She scoffed and answered, this time making sure she didn't say it aloud, 'Look who's talking about brains.'

'Shut up, I'm not your brain. I'm just inside it.'

'Who are you? A ghost who invades people's brains? Get out of my brain.' She thought to herself. She felt stupid arguing with her brain, or at least someone in her brain like the voice claimed.

'I'm you. Just better. I'm perfect.'

'I'm you. Just better. I'm perfect.' She mimicked the voice. She found her hand reaching for the glass of water which soon splashed on her face.

'What was that for?' She asked the voice but got no reply.

'You okay, honey?' Her mother looked concerned.

'Yeah, yes I am. I'm fine,' she breathed. She just nodded and went to wash the dishes. Amaira went back to her room.

'It's time you show yourself, ghost in my brain,' she said once she closed the door to her room. She didn't get a reply. 'Hello? You don't speak when I ask you to.'

'Go to the mirror,' she heard the voice say.

She did as she was told. She knew it wasn't her reflection in the mirror. She was a lot slimmer, and a lot prettier too. The voice wasn't lying when it had said it was perfect. The reflection truly was. That explained the blinking of her reflection earlier. 'Who are you?' Amaira whispered, touching the mirror with her soft hands. 'I told you, I'm a better version of you,' the reflection replied. The mirror didn't act like one. It was like it had been turned into a window. The reflection was moving around while Amaira simply stood there. Suddenly she felt a sharp throb in her head, the world went white for a second. Then it was back to normal again. 'I'm back.' Her brain said.

'Get out! I don't want a mirror reflection inside my mind.'

'Aren't you tired of being the one everyone always scolds? Aren't you? Don't you want to be known as the perfect one? Why does it have to be Saanvi or Rekha?' The voice spoke. Now that she thought about it, Amaira did want a normal life where everyone treated her well. She nodded unconsciously.

'Good. Then let me take over you. Let me control you and make you the one everyone likes.'

'Okay.' Amaira watched as her legs took her to bed. She instantly fell asleep.

She woke up with a splitting headache. 'Amaira, you're up yet? You have school today, remember?' Her mother shouted from outside the room.

'Mom, I don't want to g– I will wake up, mom,' she said. Her mother was surprised, and so was she. Until she remembered she had someone living in her brain.

She got out of bed with a light head, dreading going to school. But her ego took over. She wanted to become the best.

'Bye mom, I'm leaving!' she said, holding a slice of bread in her mouth.

She walked to school with a clear mind, knowing that her perfect self will correct her.

And it did. She improved in drawing (which she was bad at, just like any other subject), and sports and she also argued back with Saanvi and Rekha. Which she never dared to do. Her classmates started to accept her as one of their own, they even included her in the Truth or Dare game they always played. But Saanvi and Rekha hated this new form of hers. Perhaps because they were jealous. They tried to harm her more. *(Keyword*—tried. *Amaira only held them back with the strength she had.)*

This continued for two weeks, and everyone seemed to be fond of her.

Amaira sat at her study table—her body in her room, her mind someplace else. *'You are being stubborn again. One minute I stop controlling you and you're already somewhere else.'*

'You just love the word stubborn, don't you?' She asked her brain.

'I love it when I'm the one calling you stubborn. Forget that. I think it's finally time for you to control yourself. I've stayed long enough now and trust me, your nerves stink.'

'You can smell my nerves? That's disgusting,' she hissed.

'Not the point. I mean half the point but NOT the point,' the voice said.

'Well, then what's the point?'

'I want you to be you. Not me.'

'You do realize we're technically the same, right?'

'We aren't, actually. I'm the better version.' Amaira groaned at that.

'Yeah, yeah, Miss perfect.' She rolled her eyes.

'It's time for me to leave your mind.' The voice insisted.

"But people are so nice to me. They would hate me if I turn back to normal again. I can't lose you. It's like saying Superman lost his ability to fight."

'So you used me? I was just a way to get people to like you?' The voice angered.

"Wasn't that why you invaded my brain in the first place?"

'I wanted a friend, Amaira. Believe me, this might sound stupid, but being locked up in a mirror is not fun. You know what, forget it. I'll be in your mind for as long as you want. You're my "master" after all,' she enraged. Amaira didn't speak as guilt took over her.

Amaira knew she didn't feel like herself. She knew she wasn't the one gaining the courage to do everything. 'Hey,' she whispered to her head when she was in the washroom at school the next day.

'Miss perfect, you there?' She tapped her head. The voice in her head hummed in response.

'As much of an arrogant little witch you are, I'm thankful to you. You made me realize that with just a little courage I could completely change what people thought about me. Except for those two brats.' At this point, she didn't care about the looks people shot her as they passed by her talking to herself. 'I don't think I need you anymore. I'm sorry for yesterday, I shouldn't have used you like that. I'll be good from now and I'll make sure you don't get in my brain again. Feel free to talk to me from the mirrors.'

'Aww, but it's hardly been a month. I enjoyed controlling you.'

Amaira chuckled. 'I question your mood changes. Come out,' she said.

Her head throbbed once more until she opened her eyes and looked at the mirror in front of her. 'Thank you again.'

The mirror self-waved at her. 'Go,' Amaira said impatiently when the mirror self wouldn't stop waving.

'Geez, okay. But seriously, I'm proud of you. Until next time, then!' The reflection replied and disappeared, leaving Amaira to look at her imperfect self. 'I like me,' she declared. 'No, I love me.' She walked out of the washroom with pride. No one even noticed the difference in her attitude. She was her perfect self.

The Neck of the Woods

Meet the Editor

Anushree Gupta is a die-hard bookworm and an aspiring computer scientist who has a knack for scribbling poetry that romanticises life. She enjoys witty wordplay, binge-worthy book tropes and a good deal of poetic devices in her preferred reads- and her writings.

Besides her Big Three- reading, writing, and reading again, she dabbles in baking everything-chocolate, coding and watching reality TV baking shows. She has previously published her poetry on blog sites and anthologies, and believes in pushing herself to do more with everything she writes.

Drop her a hello on Instagram @incomplete_.thoughts.

Editor's Note

I thought a lot about the concept of memories while compiling these verses. That strong feeling of nostalgia when you open an old photo album, when you reread an old favourite book and see it in a whole new light- that is the feeling I have tried to encapture.

My favourite way to read these poems is like driving down a long and dusty road and stopping for breaks at different stops- I'd go straight and in order.

Our first stop is Bright, so don't forget a cold sip of iced tea.

We drive forth to encounter Rain, a cup of chai or coffee will warm you right up.

Finally a silent street, dusk falls, hang on tight to your seats.

Safe travels, and don't forget to look around and see what you might find in your neck of the woods.

~Anushree Gupta

Flowers in My Hair

Tejase Rathod

Oh, how beguiling oleanders appear,
how much I want them to adorn my hair.
Yet how poisonous they can be,
can cause such terrible agony.

Oh, look how innocuous a simple periwinkle is,
unfolding in itself,
a tender, delicate bliss.
How beautiful and real,
inside and out,
and harmless in my hair,
without a doubt.

A Bag Full of Bougainvillea

Shaymi Shah

It's been months since I've been outside
So today, I finally decide to go for a ride.
Driving towards the suburbs that dot the city's periphery
I begin to remember how nature always inspires me.
Maybe that's why I was feeling so lost lately
For nature had been calling, but I wasn't listening.

I put on some music and roll down the windows to see
the leaves rustling and dancing with the wind.
Lush green landscapes come into view
On the sides of the roads that I'm passing through
A sense of peace begins to get restored
My mind feels like it is regaining control.

The Neck of the Woods

As I take the next turn to my right,
I find myself dumbstruck and surprised.
In front of my eyes, I see
the brown, sandy land filled with colourful fallen leaves.
I wait in silence for a few minutes,
As I see how endless farmlands surround me,
and from within those browns and greens,
I see the bougainvillea trees standing so gloriously.
I find myself instantly wondering
about the captivating presence of these lovely beauties
of similar colours, in different densities
How they make us pause and fight our anxieties.

Imagine, if every flower that ever bloomed
or every plant that ever grew
were just as pretty as these bougainvillea trees
Would we be able to appreciate their beauty,
and fall in love with them just as equally?
How do these same trees have leaves
of colours ranging from white to purple and orange to pink?
To create different shades of the same colour
Do the leaves follow an underlying order?
The beautiful differences they carry within their similarities
help them face complexities, and create so many varieties,
making them stand out within landscapes and cities.

They teach us how being adaptive
can help us to survive in ways that are effective
in situations which would otherwise hold us captive.
They don't resist the change their lives bring
So why should we?

As I keep those bougainvillea leaves in my bag
take them home and preserve them in my dairy
I realize that if we preserve those precious moments
that make us feel alive in nature's presence
in our mind's diary, we can keep them alive in our memory.

The Blank Canvas

Mridini Borate

Standing near the seashore
Feeling the breeze in my hair
Staring at the blank canvas
with confusion in my head.

Running barefoot in the forest
Pure air in my lungs
My mind is enigmatic
Yet I feel so ecstatic.

After a long day,
I finally pick my brushes
and paint without any logic
This experience is entirely magic.

Fragile

Sanskriti Jain

And dear little mother of nature,
When I look at the tree.

I see souls transpiring
And love, finding its abode in its neck.

I see bodies decaying
And the cycle of life, finding its way back to Earth.

I see a hanging branch
And fragility finding its existence in me.

My Location

Ammarah Safaa

As raindrops shy away from my windowpane,
I wonder about being in pain,
in the way worlds are left in vain.

Oh, what it is to rejoice,
when we use our voices,
and paint our life with strokes of joy.

I am where the sky meets the sea,
surrounded by the breeze,
engulfed in the ease provided by thee.

Rain Again

Mridini Borate

There comes the soothing breeze of rain
which makes me forget all my pain.

It brings me back to the forgotten lane
Where I can see myself in the hall of fame.

Happiness came back to me again
And I could feel the stardust in my veins.

Alas! But something stopped the rain
I woke in my bed just the same
just to realize that it was my dream again.

Melody

Mihai Cojocaru

From far, far away, it came to distribute
a message. That mild breeze was gently dancing
around chaotically. It was announcing
a defined arrival, a kind contribute.

The breeze was bringing nature's attribute
of bountiful growth. Soon, raindrops were bouncing
far and wide. The drops were clumsily piercing
the mundane, offering a pleasant tribute.

With great ambition,
the rain'll unsettle any
normal condition.

It will bring many
new changes in addition
to some company.

Tantrum

Mihai Cojocaru

It was a sunny day when all of it commenced
A few clouds were covering the landscape
At first, the wind had no particular shape
Eventually, it began to be misplaced, rough and untamed.

The first drops were introduced by the rapid winds
Then they began to form a thick drape
Soon enough, the raindrops were larger than grapes.

There is no raft to discover
only that wild dominant event.
Within that chaos, no cover is stable.

Rain, what an untameable element.
One just stays and hopes for it to be over.
A ruler of the environment.

Inconvenience

Mihai Cojocaru

Rain, rain, rain... Rain!
A magical frame in time, right?
Says who? Who has such a blurry sight?
Rain... What a pain!

This marvel has been mystified again and again.
Rain, the bringer of peace and dim light.
Nature's golden muse, full of delight.
This deception, I must explain.

The rain, it's just a curse, that's its hidden reality.
It forces a delay in actions.
It damages the day-to-day continuity.

To prevent this illness, we need to find solutions.
I can't stand no more this rain insanity.

The Wait is Long

Rakshana Ramamurthi

Sitting by the door
Leaning against the wall
She watched the rain
Her cold fingers just peeping out of the long sleeves
Holding a hot cup of chai.

She took her first sip
Her eyes stared blankly at the sky
The smell of the rain,
and the perfect cup of chai
made her lips curve into a gentle smile.

Yet

There he was

Successfully conquering her thoughts another day,

Was it the time he used to walk with her

Or when he caught her smiling right after she rolled her eyes?

Maybe it was his forehead frown

Or the ever-so-beautiful smile showing his crooked teeth

She couldn't keep track

For there were so many.

Her feet were cold

and her heart heavy

Curling her toes under, wiping the tear off her cheek

She heaved a sigh and reminded herself

Soon. Very soon.

Captured Freedom

Ammarah Safaa

Walking on the dark, dusted road
I see the stubborn little toad,
sitting peacefully in his abode.

I feel my heart thumping fast,
while looking around the foggy vast.

The wanderlust in me screamed to be free
to be lost in the shimmering sea.

So here I am, far and alone,
with all the faces I have worn.

To Walk in Broken Limbs

Halo Golwin

There they stood by the tree in aching awe,
absorbing its hues, suffusing all.

With rays of light that scattered
across her tangled tapestry,
everything seemed to matter
when she spoke nothing of tragedy.

Gently in my slumber,
they bestowed seeds of gold.
Deaf amongst tenebrous thunder,
I awaited as the world unfold.

She sang me a lullaby,
with roots holding earth and sky.

My journey has not yet begun,
But soon will I fly
so wondrous high,
and someday meet the seraphic sun.

But if they set her ablaze once,
with ashes astray,
nothing gold is left to stay.

Hurriedly, in their prison,
they spoke the language of change.
Blind amongst sacred seasons,
the world became harsh and strange.

With shadows that flicker
across the moss-laden ground,
nothing seemed to matter
once lost in sight and sound.

My journey has not yet begun,
but soon will I walk
in broken limbs,
and someday meet a fate I can't outrun.

There they stood by the tree in disbelief,
for she has always shared my pain and grief.

Even as her flowers weep and decay,
I still blossomed in dismay.

Even as her limbs buckle and writhe,
I still avoided death's scythe.

Even as her roots burn and wither,
I still bled crimson a river.

The ash tree laments her fallen paradise,
with leaves burning in fire and ice.

But if she had to perish twice,
with disasters astray,
no one's future is left to stay.

Societal

Constraints

Meet the Editor

Vaishnavi Singh Rajput is pursuing law, she believes that expressing oneself is the most beautiful thing that God has given to everyone. And the ability to use words to express one's feelings to the outside world is a highly coveted skill.

She is a professional writer who has had her work published in over 5 anthologies and has written an entire book titled "Be Obdurate and Let Others Make Noise." As the old saying goes, "Grab the opportunity from the start." She wholeheartedly concurs. As a result, she is constantly focused and committed to her work.

She enjoys expressing herself through writing, consequently, she is a writer. Her other passions include dance which provides her peace and delight, her next interests are reading nonfiction books and listening to music.

Editor's Note

"De tribulationale ad stellas" is a Latin phrase that means "from hardship to start," and it perfectly describes our existence. We are so constrained by the walls of society that we forget to put ourselves first. The anthology's "Societal Constraint" unites us all by learning how one has to face barriers, how one has to conquer this, and how they have to outshine the world by smashing all the walls and hurdles created by these societies. I put so much heart into bringing this portion since it is relatable to all of us, and we can easily understand how we pay more attention to the society by allowing itself to become the ultimate loser as a whole. Therefore, to conquer the stars, we must first overcome obstacles and outshine the rest of the earth.

~Vaishnavi Singh Rajput

The Right and The Wrong

Neeraja Krishnaswami

Can't voice it out loud,
Can't keep it hidden.
Call it shameless or call it rude
Call it whatever you may!
Throbbing with pain
Or failing in persuading the rough
Are these the issues that we are left to deal with?
Which becomes the meaning of life?
If it is wrong to voice out pain
And it is wrong to persuade the rough,
Then the view of the world is also wrong.
And the mindset of people, too,
We set out to change
And in turn, that changes us altogether
And so do the boundaries of
The right and the wrong!

Our Existence

Neeraja Krishnaswami

What is the relation of light with darkness?
What is the relation of distances
with the ones who have distanced you?
Doesn't changing the direction seem right?
Doesn't cooking on low flame seem right?
Don't words that come out into the open seem right?
Don't unspoken words remain unspoken?
Will all these thoughts ever come to light?
Even if the heart wants to shed
these thoughts onto the near and dear
What is the folly of the person
If those near and dear
Don't understand the depth of your talk?
Re-iteration seems the only way out
And re-iteration may ease the tension
Or may complicate the situation.

But the motto is to ease the turmoil in the mind
To ease the confusion, reach the solution,
To ebb the flow, to calm the storm,
Moving the sight and the mind in that direction,
Seems the only possibility!
But will keeping quiet calm the storm?
Or will speaking out change the situation?

If someone has learned to talk
And that very fact pricks another
And the debate on this also ignites a spark

Then the beating heart of the one talking
Senses only stopping and deem it fit as the only option
Whatever the age, the culture
Relations do not pave the way forward
The thought follows to go away someplace far
Away from everything
To kindle the reality, purpose, and essence—
of our existence.

A Letter to Politicians

Arshpreet Kaur

Dear politicians,
It's a humble request,
kindly leave us to live our way.
For a very long time,
we were suffering from pain,
We just recuperated and revived from the pain,
But why, why did you spoil everything again?
Your stubborn behaviour and
your atrocious ways
Murdered many lives,
Closed our leeway.

Why can't you understand common people's soreness?
You are just sitting on a chair and playing evil games,
As you know you are safe in your Z cave,
No one even touches your shade,
But why you are making us X,

Just for your quench?
At once glanced, you changed the day,
The blue open sky turned into
The smoke of hell,
The blissful morning where
birds were chirping
And dancing in their ways,
converted into a huge explosion of waves.
The kindergarten where little angels were played,
They all vanished as you
destroyed their place
and made it battle space.
The cold winter melting because of fire flames.
The joyful vibes switched into bloodshed.
The wonderful city
rotated into the silence of graveyards.

Everywhere mangled ways.
Some die of hunger, some are killed by shells,
Some are evacuated, some are still stranded here,
Some are giving birth to endorsee,
During this horror phase.
For you, war is a game,
but ask them who lost their loved ones in a day.
A mother lost her son,

A son lost his dad,
A wife who designed a beautiful life with her mate,
You snatched her fate.
Those who are born to complete their family,
You made them alone.
You shattered their dreams,
You extinguished their fortune.
Just to satisfy your ego,
You played such a horrendous game.
I think you are a demon, in a layer of humans.
In history, you must be unforgivable.
Whatever it is, no one can return our loved ones.
No one can heal our aches,

Though we have hearts,
Inside, they are pale.
Many torment souls,
wandering here and there
And incessantly cursing you which will become
nightmare for you.
You will never live a serene life
because you are responsible for this genocide,
this genocide.

Travesty of an Afghani Woman

Arshpreet Kaur

I was an exuberant young girl,
Who had great desires to fly
And touch the sky.
But this moment was ephemeral for me,
No more dreams are being existing,
As few vindictive men have broken my wings.
Every moment was halcyon for me,
Now my life is going to be miserly.
And don't try to convince me that,
Something good in His every step,
The actual truth is something else.
Now I am crotchety if someone is saying,
God has some ulterior motive behind that.
All words seem useless,
The world is an evil place.
Now I count as a petty object and
That's just for carnal desires.

Those monsters have such bloody hungriness.
Even, if they are not leaving dead.
Just for making themselves relax,
They are erasing their itchiness.
Those days were grandeur for me,
When I kicked my sphere on the field,
Now they kicked me inside the dark hole
And trying to weave my own.
I have to burn each and every endeavor,
Which I earned with my seek.
I buried my degrees, buried my aims.
Even I covered myself with a black sheet.
Everything flashed before my eyes,
No longer laughing, no longer songs,
I no longer meet my friends
And no more my favorite yellow dress
With red lipstick and black nail paint.
Streets are vacuous, markets are dry,
Sometime before, which were flush with life.
It makes me blue, no one is ready to stand beside me.
Tyranny is that all mighty powers are muted here.

Apathy is that even I thought ready to dart,
Want to leave my land and
Join the crowd which is going to evacuate.
Suddenly something erupted there,
All are running and it seems someone has chased
The swarm of insects.
All around smoke is there, along with pieces of the dead.
Echo of screams, blood is everywhere.
I think I am no more there,
I have chosen the freedom of the soul
Rather than soul-dead.

What is 'Life'

Riya Varshney

Life in simple words?
Everyone will have different answers.
Some will say that life is a journey, some will say that life is a game.
Everyone has a different point of view to see and live.

According to me, life is a game, playing which we have to reach the destinations called happiness through obstacles called sorrows. This game starts with our arrival in this world and ends after we die. While playing the game, we come across some players who demoralize us and some who help us in playing the game—but such people are very difficult to get along with. While playing sports, we reach such a stage. Where we need a good and true, companion who supports us at every step, or in other words we need a companion. How the whole life (game) gets completed with him is not known. If the partner is good then every step is easily crossed. Sometimes there are moments where we give up, thinking 'It's all over now, but we don't know that we have started a new story. Some stories of most people are incomplete hat let's start a new story. One decision either right or wrong can change the whole life. If there is sorrow in life, then there is happiness somewhere, the only difference is that sorrow is an uninvited guest and happiness has to be invited. Some people believe that one of the goals of life is to make the people around you happy, because if they are happy then we will be happy. This is not wrong, but I would like to move the words back and forth a bit, I believe 'if we are happy then we will be able to keep the people around us happy.' There is no one goal in life, everyone has different goals, huh. When one goal is accomplished, another bigger goal is ready for him. But nowadays, money is everything, those who have it, have lived the life we have, and those who do not have any, eat stumbling blocks from rate to rate. This is wrong, isn't it? After all, if there is a rich person and a poor person, why are the rich only on based money? Living life is said to be where one gets two times of bread, family support, and a peaceful night's sleep. Where do the rich get peace at night, they have a fear. Well this also, happened to be a life. That's how the game of life ends. The one who has got the sole support of family, happiness, and peace, in the true sense, is a game of life.

Being 378 Times Inferior to Her

Anushka Verma

Gold wraps and gleams in her hair,
From beginning to end mine is black,
I desire my skin to be 15 shades fairer,
Akin to her, melanin is what I crave to lack.
They are wonderstruck by her enchanting
bright pink lips,
For a duration of 365 days,
7 hours in only when she weeps,
Scar free body augments her magnificent
elegance by 17 times,
And that's how on me she unintentionally
cloudbursts sour limes.
The words engraved by her on paper feel like royalty to read,
But mine seems to suffer from
dwarfism in front of those,
I am treated as dangerous,
nefarious thorns,

While she is treated as grandly as
the petals on a rose.
She has sorted the best ways and rules
and abides by them,
Which is sure to succeed at once and bring
her loads of fame,
But I haven't even figured out my aim,
Then how can I be liberated from pools of shame?
We both dream and tie ropes to
the same aristocratic dreams,
Among which some of mine are insuperable
for the ones who never tried but supreme,
The only difference is that she has more government notes,
And the confidence she wears
will bring her more votes.
I want to have all the royalty that she possesses,
I want government notes, books, and gorgeous dresses.
When I want to be her, I kill my real self and die,
I become another her and to the supreme energy, I lie.

I lose my identity, I become a Xerox,
I become black and white and lose all my rainbow tint,
I stab myself and hit my creativity with rocks,
That makes them know all deep
secrets with a simple hint.
Yes, we forget that beauty ain't
anything but being ourselves,
Beauty is contained in everything
like the books on the shelves,
We are beautiful in our bodies and flaws,
Let's not be someone else for this sabotage cause.
There's beauty in being lost,
There's beauty in warm tears,
There's beauty in our self-frost,
There's a hidden beauty in our fears.
There's beauty in having the hair
tint that you aren't appeased by,
The beauty in painful written truth shines
more than the greatest happy lie,
There's beauty in feeling inferiority
before it widens to superiority,
There's beauty when you are the only one to face
the challenges faced by a tree.

There's beauty to learn under
candle flames at night,
Royalty is getting scars after
the bloodiest fight.
Yes, these insecurities play a great
role in defining us,
As we fought these dilemmas without creating a fuss,
And we will be remembered and etched with
gold and diamonds in history,
For where we previously were 378 times
inferior, and where we will be.

The Unstoppable You and Your Self-Worth

Komal Joshi

They say to sit, talk and
behave according to society and
it's the norm but isn't that unfair and just wrong!?
I say let's dream,
go on an adventure and explore life and
yourself a little more!
Live life your way, and love yourself the way you should be
loved! Don't worry about what others think
and say just follow your heart and soul else you'll regret it all on
your deathbed Thinking how I had the opportunities,
all those options, and my own desires
and dreams but I was too scared and
worried to take a chance... thinking what if I fail?

What if society fails to understand and accepts me
and my decisions? Am I not good enough?
Am I not worthy enough? What
if this and what if that…

But I say let's go a little crazy,
let's go a little carefree and a little happier for the world needs more
of that, you see Happier, positive and
compassionate you is simply the
best you that you can be
So, set your spirits high, smile more,
put your worries
on the low because you my friend are a true asset
and a beautiful gift to the world just the way you are!
The world I came and saw,
I thought hang on... more happiness,
positivity, smiles, laughter,
hope, realness, and peace are wanted and so needed
in today's day and age
Don't you simply agree with me, my friend?
So why not be the best version of yourself that the world
is yet to see The real raw unfiltered and beautiful you that's
carefree!

Hope

Mukunda Maheshwari

Let's hope we cope,
Hope is a might,
A might brings up a light,
A light clears all our doubts and fright.

Be a grass or a tree,
It's a matter of how you see,
This world is so vast,
No problem what you are.

The actual power lies within your heart,
Have the energy to find on the bloody start,
A setback gives rise to a comeback,
No matter what you are,
Just be the best in what you are.

I Tried

Anvi Gupta

I tried but could not succeed
I cried inside but, no one did read.
It was the first time I kept everything to myself—
I screamed but found everyone was deaf.

I wanted to go away. Wanted to free them--
But was afraid of them keeping their minds in the mayhem.
I was never strong enough to do that
However, made a decision and continued to detract.

I tried but could not succeed.
I was evil back again, the way I used to be,
I lost, bent down on my knees--
Didn't feel anything; neither ego nor care.

"And, the bloody, hapless Devil rose", I declared!
It was a phase; now it is gone,
I have my new self on
I tried and did succeed
I worked hard and felt the need
Of not going down again
But rising. Amen

The Prize

Tejaswini Mittal

They look at her
With those vicious grins
Not realizing that
She's broken within

She cowers back
Trying to disappear
Hoping that, for once,
They'll go easy on her

But they don't,
They never do
The onlookers enjoy the show
Laughing along with the Devil's crew

Pelting against her invisible armour
The hail of insults begins
They call her ugly, they call her fat
Even when she's beautiful, even when she's thin

What they don't know
Is the effect their words have
She stopped eating long ago
Now she starves herself

She cakes her face with makeup
Every day, when she doesn't need to
Hoping to look pretty
Not realizing she's already beautiful

They shove her and push her around
Just wanting to have some fun
They pull at her clothes and laugh
Yanking at her hair, undone

"Her clothes are disgusting,
Her hair's a mess,"
They laugh, and she wails
Unable to suppress it

Finally, they're bored
Had their fill for the day
She runs home, never stopping
The tears running down her face

Reaching the front door
She feigns a smile
Her family is unaware of
What goes on in her life

She hurries up the stairs
Towards her room
And locks the door
With a single thought, she's consumed

Opening her drawer
She takes out the blade
She wastes no time
Glides it across her wrist once again

It hurts and it burns
But she doesn't make a sound
She's now numb to the pain
There's no sign of a frown

Impassive, she sighs
Wanting to end her misery
Once and for all
She wants to be free

So she continues
This time, pressing harder
Wanting to cut a vein
She presses the blade further

Tears streaming down her face
She smiles
She doesn't have to wait much longer
Just a little while

And now she's gone
And now they realize
The impact of their words
What a wonderful prize

They used to laugh
But now they frown
Now they ask themselves,
"What have we done?"

A Girl's Perspective

Arpita Mukherjee

"Leave the job and get married"—It is usually the only solution to all issues a 21st century girl faces after a long hectic day at work. Even if, by mistake, she shares a problem, conventional minds start lecturing her about safety, security, family reputation, and whatnot. Is marriage the only resort for all her daily issues? Is she ever asked whether she is ready for it or not? What if she is left with her biggest dream not yet fulfilled? Does that matter? After all, she is a girl, who cares? Her existence is always considered unsafe in our society. What if something misfortunate happens to her? Her disappearance is acceptable if her appearance is ugly. Who would marry her? Better get rid of this burden of flesh soon!

The girl marries the boy chosen by her parents dreaming of a secure life full of bliss and joy. She compromises her independence to focus on a new unplanned beginning. Now all her decisions depend on someone's office timings or school vacations. Her little wants to basic needs wait for someone's acceptance and permission. Her character certificate is subject to the mood of a few bigmouths.

But is she really happy with all that she has? Has marriage been the troubleshooter to all her misfortunes? Has the burden been lifted from the shoulder of our so-called "cultured society"? Have they succeeded in making her life any better? Food for thought!

How do you forget to love yourself?

Dr. Varsha

Does the sun forget to rise?
Does the earth forget to rotate?
Do the flowers forget to bloom?
Then my darling,
how do you forget
to love yourself?

Our body is a divine creation
Change cannot diminish its beauty
People will come, people will go
Loving yourself is only your duty

Love, in itself, is a beautiful experience
If it stood against the world in war everything else
would be nothing but dust
as compared to love
Who can share love or sell it?

In the end, all that matters
is that you love yourself
and this love is immortal
and forever eternal

The Darkness

Sandhita Agarwal

You try to touch what you can't see
You can feel it when you're with me
You pretend to make friends with it
The darkness that's inside me

You baptized it in your turbulent seas
A name so vile was never meant to be
You tried to stamp it out of me
The darkness that was me

You smothered it with your murderous hands
Left in the dust to rot and turn rank
Till it rose out of the ashes, a phoenix to be
The darkness that was in me

It's become my armour, my elixir of life
To fight against you and your demons tonight
Your demons are a horde of fiends
Your darkness is a swallowing abyss

Your legions have been vanquished
Your demons have been slayed
May you live forever and ever
And your sins follow in your wake

I swallow back my darkness in a giant gulp
Sending it back to the cradle in my bosom
It lights up all my nights these days
And keeps other demons at bay.

The Life

Sandhita Agarwal

She sat at the end of the bar
Their eyes twinkling a story on her lips
All around her glasses were tinkling
I sat huddled over my beer and chips
She started narrating her merry tales
Of her endless conquests and burnt sails
Of the ones she poked and pushed
And the ones that had her ambushed

The crowd around her listened enthralled
I sat in the corner with my head hung down
Her voice now reaching an unnatural crescendo
Her easiest victory, her unworthiest foe

The one she didn't even need to touch
The one who toppled over on their own
Roars escaped her laboured lungs
She banged her fists on the table

Tears of mirth rolled down her cheeks
The crowd collectively let out delightful shrieks
She suddenly turned toward me
Her finger pointing accusingly

It was you; it will always be you
The crowd mimicked her as if on cue
Their laughter filled the empty night
I sat frozen in my misery and plight.

The Broken

Sandhita Agarwal

Sometimes it creaks, sometimes it chirps
Sometimes it brings me happiness
Most often a whirlpool of despair

I am broken never to be repaired
A chair in the garage waiting to be mended
It doesn't realize it won't be tended

Broken by its creator, left to rot by its maker
A car that never drives freely
The cogs in the mesh never move easily

I am a child of doom and gloom
A symphony left unfinished; a house left unpainted
Inside I am an empty room, to the world I am untainted.

The Green-Eyed Monster

Claire Casapao

Nothing is small
About that green-eyed, red-haired monster
That's breaking down my walls.

Every triumph, every victory
Is the monster's analgesic.
Its scars stop hurting
But they never disappear.

Every defeat, every downfall;
Then begins the rainfall.
The monster screams and cries;
The ache never dies.

The monster feeds on hatred;
Will I ever see it dead?
The monster is overfed;
Overfed with frustration.

The monster sees red.
It would like to drop some lead
On its opponents' heads.

I see the monster every day.
Oh, how I wish there was a way
To keep it in its cage.

It might break out
At any moment with a loud shout.

I struggle to keep the monster chained inside,
But it fights to get out with all its might.
It very rarely sees the light;
It stays in the dark of the night.

But when it does get out,
Oh, 'woe is me'!
I yell, stomp, and scream

Until the monster is no longer queen.

The Saga of Her Start-up

Meet the Editor

Dr. Geetanjali Patil Pawar is passionate for books based on real-life stories which offer positivity. She is an academician working as a lead program design and construct in Edtech from Bangalore. She aspires to empower women at a grass root level and help them achieve their dreams.

Editor's Note

Women through history untold have meticulously handled their household expenses and savings for their family, be it with or without proper business knowledge. Indian women have shown their enterprising skills throughout history which goes unwritten and untold.

This theme is a saga of women start-up ventures, the story of their dreams and struggles to create their own world. Here are few bosses who have decided to share their stories filled with ups and downs. The queens who built their empire and wrote legacies worth sharing.

~Dr Geetanjali Patil Pawar

1

The Journey of My Passion

Ranjitha S, Founder, NITARA

It all began when a newspaper ad mentioned "Kathak" classes. I started wondering what this dance form was all about. Always interested in dance during school/college programmes and competitions, it struck me that it was time to take my hobby forward in an organized manner, through the world of classical dance. I went ahead, enrolled myself, and started the classes; and since then, there was no looking back. My age back then was 19. (No, it's never too late to learn any art form.)

As my journey of being a Kathak student continued, I also went on to complete my MBA in HR and joined a job, which was a 9-to-5 routine. It made me realize that it just wasn't meant for me. By this time, my love for Kathak had increased to an extent that it was not just my hobby anymore; it was my passion! I've always believed in the phrase "Whatever happens, happens for the good" as you get to learn and experience from your experiments in life, which brings clarity to what you want and what you don't, irrespective of whether you think it's good for you or not. Complicated? I don't think so. By now, I had realized that I did not enjoy a 9-to-5 routine.

As time went by, I continued to gather knowledge on Kathak, thanks to my teachers (grateful to them forever).

I started thinking, *what am I doing with all this knowledge? How else can I make it valuable? Kathak is so beautiful, there should be more people who know and learn about it. How can I spread it? And then an important thought ran through my mind. There are so many beautiful artists whom I've come across, who have learnt certain art forms by themselves and are spreading it.*

I, on the other hand, have had the privilege of learning it from my gurus to expand my knowledge, why can't I teach it to others?!

I had this desperate thought in my mind that people who are interested in Kathak should experience the beauty of it, and it should spread more. I wanted people to fall in love with Kathak, just the way I did. And yes, I wanted to help!

When you have a purpose in life, even though it's unknown to you, the Almighty guides you in various ways to help manifest the same. One day, one of my friends expressed that she wanted to learn Kathak. I thought, why not; I can teach her. Not realizing the spark of that moment or how it was going to turn out to be, we discussed and decided, 'Let's at least begin!'

And that is how, I started teaching Kathak for the very 1st time in my bedroom, with very little space. When there was a need for more space, we moved to a bigger room and moved the furniture around. Meanwhile, through word of mouth, another girl expressed her interest too. And I gladly said yes, to my 2nd unofficial student! By then, it was clear to me the enjoyment of teaching Kathak and the happiness that I felt when they would execute what has been taught! Tats it!!! I wanted to continue to teach Kathak, still unsure of what the next phase was! Yes, I quit my job and my dance classes as a student, to explore this path on my own!

It's never easy to take this kind of a decision, but you'll never know unless you give it a shot, right?! Well, I'm glad I did!

Having a blessed support system to follow your passion is a huge plus point indeed. With my amazing parents, I expressed my need for space, and they gladly agreed to build a small structure on our terrace. Picked a date, inaugurated the new space, and kicked off.

Chose the name "NITARA" for what I called an institute now. Created and updated information on social media. Word spread through friends and family, and enquiries started flowing in. Hence, I got my business cards and brochures printed. Yet another exciting moment of having my own business card, especially for something that I love. I now knew that I was an entrepreneur! The thought was life changing. I also structured a certain syllabus to be taught in an organized manner, rules, and regulations to be followed by the students, fixed the class timings etc. I started taking interviews before admitting students as many of them would mistake a dance institute for a fitness place and many other reasons too. Hence, I needed to make sure that a student who enrolled, is truly interested in dance or Art in general. I still do. Only when a student has a huge thirst for knowledge, can this journey of teaching and learning be exciting and effective.

I believe that experiencing dance is a connection of the body, mind, and soul where the body actually comes last. What your feel internally, is what the body expresses. The depth of being able to understand the concept of dance is both a mental and physical process.

The beauty of it can be truly felt when experienced in person. You need to be ready to dedicate yourself, and also do justice to it! Things were becoming clearer as I started acting upon it. For some time, my parents always thought that this might be my part-time plan and would continue to look for a 'proper job.' But as time went by, they saw how comfortable and happy I was, with what I was doing with more students flowing in, to such an extent, that they even re-did the space of the dance class into a bigger one so that I could fit in more students. I couldn't be more grateful for my loved ones to be sharing this journey with me.

At NITARA, I've had the privilege of sharing my knowledge with hundreds of students. I believe that they should be approachable to the teacher in order to enhance learning. Hence, we experience a friendly and comfortable student-teacher relationship, and yet, keep intact, the disciplinary measures that are necessary to be committed to an Art form.

'Balance' is the key!

Some important things in life that I always tell my students:

1. Self-love is extremely important in order to fall in love with what you do, and everything else.
2. Don't judge others as you do not want to be judged too, as it hampers learning.
3. Don't join an Art form just because you want to become famous. Focus on being good at what you do.
4. Humility takes an artist a long way. You should always have an attitude of "I want to learn," irrespective of your experience, rather than "I know everything."
5. You can surely see a positive aspect even in the most difficult situations of life. Allow time to heal things, rather than to give up.

The reason I involve life skills at NITARA is that dance is not just about moving your hands and legs. It's not something that you do, it's something that you are! It can be enjoyed only by understanding it and by inviting it into your life as your friend forever.

Whom would you rather spend more quality time with? A scary stranger whom you do not know, or a best friend who used to be a stranger once, but over a period of time, you just love spending time with each other. There you go!

There was a time when I did not know what Kathak was, and as of today (2023), NITARA turns 12, which is one of the biggest milestones of my life. My husband, my parents and my students are my biggest support.

And my journey continues.

At times, I've wondered why I pursued an MBA if I had to end up being an artist. But I've never regretted anything that has happened in my life. All the dots in our lives join together to lead us to beautiful places and rewards. During my job as an HR, I was forced to polish my communication and people skills which definitely helped me when I had to deal with so many students at NITARA. When I look back, I have one prominent feeling; Gratitude!

All those of you who have had thoughts about taking your passion forward, I would say: GO FOR IT! Do not worry about the result. May the journey help you embrace and reveal your inner self, irrespective of the result!

IF I CAN DO IT, SO CAN YOU!

2

Catharsis—Collection of Smiles

Ranjini Sasidharan, Director Catharsis

Trees, twigs, leaves, seeds, and stones always fascinated me since Childhood. My collection box would be filled with these things picked from parks and roads. I grew up admiring them. My peers always found me weird, and I was always asked "What is so fascinating about the things I picked?" I was the black sheep of the flock during my elementary school days. I barely knew that I would not be going to become a doctor or an engineer or work in banks. Becoming an Artist was never considered a profession in my family. My high school summer vacation was so dreadful, all my friends would go off to native places. Absolutely no connection with anyone. The good old days had no phones. It gave me a lot of time to explore art, I spent most of my time drawing and painting. My best friend's sister was the only artist I had ever seen, and I admired her so much. I wanted to paint like her. I wanted to be an artist. With a lot of effort, I gather the courage to convince my parents to go to the College of Fine Arts. The adventure started there; I found my flock of black sheep there. Everyone was amused by something or the other. Though everyone had a different muse, all had one thing in common—all were different. I had a lot of opportunities to observe the masters, research, interact, meet, and have long discussions. As I evolved through it, I met many people who were practising art in many different ways. To me, art was no more about making some paintings and putting up a show in a gallery but there was more to explore. I continued to meet many artists and attend different workshops. I thoroughly enjoyed the intellectual talks and discussions.

Years passed, and I took up a job, worked as a designer, as an art teacher and also set up a preschool along with a friend. Life moved on with work and family and kids. However, there was this time in my life I sensed a lot of loneliness, and this hit me very hard. I would not know what to do. Where to go? Whom to seek help from? In pursuit of getting out of it and knowing more, I discovered something beautiful. At this point, I had not painted for more than 5 to 6yrs due to work. Out of frustration I took out my art supplies and scribbled and painted. It was so therapeutic and fun. I felt I could release so much of my stifled emotions and felt so very light. In that instant all the dots connected from the college time research, meetings, and discussions. Quoting Rumi 'what you seek is seeking you!' I kept getting invited to attend art forums. Some mentors were awesome and some I didn't enjoy much. I continued to do artwork based on this. As I painted more, colours were becoming my language of expression and my figurative/object-driven style turned into an abstract. The colours gave me strength, joy, and clarity. I realized that Art is not for only artists. Art is for everyone. Colours give the freedom of expressing one's thoughts, feelings, and emotions.

Since I was a preschool co-entrepreneur, the curriculum we designed was art dominant, I also taught art to children on weekly basis. It gave a lot of joy and learning from children and their barrier-less, no-inhibition thoughts. However, my discovery of bringing out emotions into a painting and knowing that it is an inborn skill, everyone is born with it, was giving me a high and pushing me to create something for everyone. I very strongly wanted to break the cliché of art can be made by an artist only and break the belief that art is a piece of thing to be displayed. I wanted to make people become aware that art is a language you can use beyond words. I wanted to create a platform where people would come and paint their hearts out. Maybe hold a space where they could use art as a tool to introspect themselves and recognize and acknowledge varied emotions. Sadly, art is not nurtured as a language in the schooling system but taught as a hobby.

I discussed this with a few of my friends they all acknowledged it's a brilliant idea and encouraged me to bring support to make it into a wholesome therapeutic session. I designed a module on recognizing emotions and colours. And a couple of more activities. The first session I conducted was with my preschool parents. Though the feedback was good and was impactful for a couple of parents. I felt something was missing. So took a deep dive, researched a bit more and re-designed the workshop. A much more detailed and step-by-step process. Keeping all challenges, I faced in the previous session. I wanted it to be a whole day session. Where every participant is away from the day-to-day noise and challenges. I didn't want to conduct these workshops as art workshops but as something beyond. I wanted it to be a totally cathartic experience. That's how the word Catharsis became the name of the workshop. Going forward I felt something more was required to conclude the workshop. I wanted the participant to feel that they had gifted a day for themselves, and they go back home relaxed and refreshed. A dear friend Sunitha and my co-partner at the preschool were practising touch healing. As we were discussing the workshop, we realized healing would be the best way to conclude a day's session. So, we were up and ready with the Catharsis workshop to present. Together we decided to borrow from our best experience to create wholesome programs that provide a platform to introspect through the medium of art and mindfulness that help people rapidly learn and adapt life skills to ease out complex challenges in life. We conducted this workshop with a few of our dear friends. We hosted it in a place away from the clamour, amidst nature. It was a beautiful Sunday and lovely weather and dear friends as participants in our workshop. It was a magical day. We gather the best feedback and kept working and kept bettering as we conducted more workshops.

Every Catharsis workshop was so fulfilling and so satisfying. We have conducted it with more friends, family, parents etc. Slowly the word of mouth spread, and our program started getting to know more people. We have had an amazing journey conducting these workshops sometimes in groups, sometimes with only couples, and sometimes one with one personal session. We had different kinds of people participating; some were art lovers, some were artists, and some were first timers. We witnessed people breaking their barriers of 'can't…' and making it possible, some painted their stories, some poured out their sufferings, some painted joy, some painted gratitude, some painted forgiveness, some let go of past hurt, and some created a new beginning. Some splashed colours, some drew, some used only one colour, and some used all the colours. Each workshop is so special and has left such a vivid memory. As we explored doing more workshops, we got more creative and more different modules were created. Amazing revelations and transforming experiences to treasure, both for us and for the participants. It's been 8 years since we have done these workshops with close to 600 people.

On the other side Catharsis as a Firm opened up more different possibilities. We created more modules, we created paint parties where a group of people catch up over a cup of tea/coffee and paint for fun, and we created teambuilding workshops called Meraki where the entire office crowd would experience the nuance of the team through art, and we even created Mural workshops for corporates where the entire team would paint the office wall. We created community-building activities, and as a community, we painted the street, it was like a festival the youngest as young as 2 years old to the oldest as old as 80-year-olds, all with paints and brushes pouring out joy and creativity. So far more than 300 people have experienced different forms of Catharsis.

My joy knew no bounds when I saw all of them having fun and

expressing themselves. My thought, my belief that Art is an inborn skill, that art is a language of expression, art is a language of introspection, Art is not just for Artist but for everyone became true. I realized my purpose for choosing to become an artist was not just to paint a few canvases, it was beyond that. My truth is that I am a gifted person, and my gift is to gift the language of colours, and feelings of colours to one and all. Today I stand being so grateful to all of them who gave me an opportunity and trusted me to give them this experience. Catharsis is an invitation to discover the self, let go of the baggage, enjoy the process of life, envision, and manifest desires and just have fun with colours.

3

The Dreamweaver

Deepali Shital Gotadke
Founder and Business Owner,
WebDreams India and ClickHubli.com

Today I got up a little late as I could not sleep the whole night; I feared getting left behind the technology. I started getting nausea again as this is the sixth month of the pregnancy. Every day I was worried that this gap of almost two years would make me unemployable. This thought comes to all the women who plan for a child and take a long break.

This is the story of me, a simple girl from a second-tier city of Karnataka, Hubli. I completed my computer science engineering from the well-known Walchand College of Engineering, Sangli. I did my primary and secondary schooling at a Marathi medium school. I wanted to become a doctor but missed my medical seat by just two marks. After my marriage in the year 1996, I came to Hubli. I could not speak Kannada at that time and joined Kannada tuitions; soon, I became proficient in Kannada reading and writing. I always had a passion for making a mark in my field. Initially, I started working with my husband and developed accounting, billing, and office management software for our family business in the year 1996. In the year 1997, after the birth of my son, within 40 days, I joined as a lecturer in an engineering college to gain knowledge of the internet. I was always worried that I would be out of the ever-changing IT field if I take a long break. I was fascinated by the technology which has reached my doorstep through the internet. When my husband asked me what I wanted as a gift, I asked for "3 months of an internet connection"!

In 1998, with my one-year-old baby, I started studying internet technologies and e-commerce. I wanted to do something online to help me establish my identity while managing my family responsibilities. I worked in our engineering college as a lecturer after my graduation. I was instrumental in starting a computer institute where I worked as a program director and designed even the course material. I always felt the need to upgrade my knowledge, I wanted to have work experience in some IT company, so in the year 2000, I went to Pune, stayed there for four months, and joined a small IT firm. I got practical experience at a web design company. In the same year, I got an opportunity to travel to the United States of America; I saw that people use the internet to buy products online. I was fascinated by *e-commerce.* I felt this technology is soon going to change the world. As e-commerce provides the comforts of buying from home, many consumers will quickly change how they buy and start buying online.

I started thinking and studying about e-commerce. I wanted to start a service for NRIs and others who wish to send fresh flowers and cakes to their near and dear ones in other cities. When I talked about this with my family and friends, nobody endorsed my idea. Still, the idea of launching an e-commerce portal became stronger day by day in my mind.

ClickHubli.com is my brainchild; I registered the domain in April 2000, which was launched in December 2000. This is the first e-commerce portal from North Karnataka. Initially, I thought of selling Kasuti (hand embroidered) sarees from North Karnataka, online. This idea of selling sarees online was very new; even I could not find any model, so I decided to wear the sarees myself, shoot the photos, and launch the portal. In April 2001, I got my first order from South Africa. Then, I enhanced the portal with flowers, cakes, and many other gift options. Slowly, my network started developing across the country; initially, I was delivering only in Hubli Dharwad and surrounding areas. Later on, I engaged my cousins and friends to take care of the orders in other cities. With that, I started developing websites also and hired three people. This firm has 12 e-commerce portals like ClickRoses.com and GiftWithLuv.com, and I have a network of Florists and Bakers across the country through which the gifts and flowers can be delivered. This network has now been spread over more than 300 cities in India.

I often joined various firms from time to time; In 2003, I again became a mother. After a break of 1 year, I felt that I have to upgrade my knowledge. I joined KLE tech university as a lecturer.

In the year 2008, I launched WebDreams which offers web design, development, and digital marketing services. With the help of a team of 12 members, I developed more than 400 websites. The firm dominated the local web design market of Hubli-Dharwad. I could get the prestigious website design work of government organizations like Hubli-Dharwad Municipal Corporation, Hubli-Dharwad Police, Northwest Karnataka State Road Corporation, Southwestern Railways, BRTS, Hubli-Dharwad Urban Development Authorities, etc. Presently Clickhubli.com and WebDreams together have more than 20000 customers.

Kasuti is the traditional art of hand embroidery from North Karnataka. I was fascinated by the artwork; I wanted to promote this art. I saw that many women from rural areas and slums do this artwork. They do not get sufficient payment for this hard work. Kasuti is a very intricate work, and a lot of time is involved in designing a saree with Kasuti work. I wanted to promote this art internationally so that these women can get paid well for their efforts.

Through ClickHubli.com, I promoted Kasuti art, and also developed an app for designing Kasuti artwork. Consumers can use this app to design their own patterns of Kasuti work on sarees or other fabrics.

My portal is top-ranked for Kasuti-related information. ClickHubli team developed a logo for *Sui Dhaaga*, a film by Yash Raj productions. Thus, we got a national reorganization for our art.

My passion is to bring more and more women entrepreneurs online and help them sell online. My goal is to mentor and empower 5000 women with e-commerce and digital marketing training, and I want to support them through my portal wesellonline.org. Through this, I have successfully trained 2750 women for Digital Marketing and selling online.

The training platform https://www.unescap.wesellonline.org/ is designed by me exclusively for Women entrepreneurs in South Asia. It concentrates on leveraging the potential of e-commerce for expanding its business. Here the women entrepreneurs receive training in e-commerce under the UNESCAP—EIF. Later they will be able to display their products on the platform, and they can also answer the queries raised by potential customers.

This platform is designed for conducting hands-on training on e-commerce and digital marketing. Once the entrepreneurs get trained, they can list their products at one of the marketplaces available in their respective countries. They can develop their platforms for conducting their business.

I have an exclusive idea to make all the participants eligible for the UNESCAP-EIF program. Here, I have provided an excellent platform and invited most women entrepreneurs to register themselves as entrepreneurs. This wonderful program made by me will provide a great door wide open for the woman entrepreneurs of all the developing countries of South Asia.

It becomes essential to understand how this wonderful idea of training them got into my mind at this stage.

I always understood that the presence of women in MSME, the

micro, small and medium enterprises, is the backbone of all sectors in the economy of South Asian countries. So, I felt let us make the best use of this opportunity where all the women who have multi-talents in them can use this platform. I believe that women, through this platform, can empower themselves socially and economically. The portal is concentrated on e-learning courses, an E-Commerce portal, e-commerce manual, which provides step by step guide to selling online. The main motto is the urge to make women independent and understand that they are a sustainable resource.

My "Just do it" and fearless attitude helped me achieve my dream; I believe that we get the fruits if we do our *Karma*. I firmly believe that everybody should dream and think big. We should set our goal, and daily we should take small steps towards it to achieve it.

Just keep in mind, keep chasing your dreams because dreams do come true.

4

It's a Beautiful Thing

Madhumathi J Dharwar

Founder, Architecture Firm

It's a beautiful thing when career and passion come together! Passion is Energy! You need to feel the power that comes from focusing on what excites you! This passion for your work is the straight path to success.

I'm a proud native of Gulbarga (now Kalaburagi), of the HK region (the so-called backward area of Karnataka), which ironically has presented the world with innumerable eminent personalities in various fields.

Securing the first rank and topping the University for my final year of Architecture, was the first feather on my cap! It was a great feeling. My mother was so happy and extremely proud of me. That's it!! That's just one part of my achievement. Having lost my dad quite early in life, we are a family of just....5 sisters, (we call ourselves. The Famous 5!) Including my Strong Mother. Being from a comparatively orthodox family and an equally sensitive and shy society, my first steps in Architecture as an Architect were restricted.

Though I joined a firm and started my job as an architect, it was just working on the table. Family restrictions made it nearly impossible for the necessary and important site visits. I had no practical knowledge. Of course, I got to learn and understand a lot from my seniors at the office, but nothing could compensate for the lack of practical/on-site knowledge.

After a couple of years, just like the usual journey of any other typical Indian lady, marriage followed. Accompanied by new challenges for life! Profession, of course, took a back seat. But somehow, just couldn't keep me off from Architecture. Circumstances forced me to stay for nearly a couple of years with my in-laws at *Basavakalyan* (taluka in Bidar district). I still managed to keep my Drawing board and T-square, active there, with small random works for friends.

After 2 years of marriage, I was now based in a metro, Hyderabad. There was enough scope for my work, but I hardly had any contacts. I joined a small Government college as a guest lecturer, to share my Book knowledge on Architecture. I was paid Rs 40/class!! (That was in 1999). I could manage 3 classes per day. That Rs 40/class, made way for my first FD, a Fixed deposit of Rs 10,000/-! Though my Better half has always pampered me and made me feel like a Queen, still, earning your own money gives you the required Self Confidence and you just feel good. Great...Worthwhile!!

After a short term with the college, I joined a Landscape firm. Again, for a short duration. My situation was like, Jack of all trades...Master of None!! I still, never let go of any opportunity to work. Accepted all sorts of works related to architecture and was meagrely paid. I would also like to add here that drawings were done free of cost, for the so-called friends/ relatives/ extended relatives.... the list is endless. (Frankly, the free service hasn't still stopped).

As the journey continued with small insignificant works, I stumbled upon a good project. (Remember, I still was sort of blank with my practical knowledge) Call it my madness, eagerness, or stupidity, I started working on the project. No miracles here!! It was a sheer disaster. I'm still not too sure, why that client of mine (A Real Gentleman), didn't stop me earlier. When I was halfway through the project, I approached him for a part of my professional fee. He just told me..." madam, do you think you deserve it?

That was it!!! Those words shook me. I was shattered and disappointed. I thought that was the end of my career!

It took me quite a long time to get over this incident. But this was also, the turning point in my professional life.

There's a one-liner, which was frequently used by one of our lecturers in college. (On a lighter note). The mistake of a doctor is buried deep into the ground, but, the mistake of an architect, is above the ground- for everyone to see".

This particular incident haunted me for long. It's a lifetime lesson, never to be forgotten. Besides, it's not the mistake that defines us...Rather. How/what we learn from them matters! They have the power to turn you into something better than you were before." It's also a fact that life's greatest lessons are usually learnt at the worst times.

I eventually, joined a firm and started interning seriously for nearly 2 years. It was now nearly 10 years since I had graduated. It was during this real internship that I started discovering the Real me! My passion towards interiors was magnetic. Was just pulled into this magical world. It was a lovely transformation. It gave me immense satisfaction to see my visuals and imagination taking shape. The result made me Happy! (Notice, this is the first time, I've used 'Happy', for myself). During the same time, I also discovered my love for small spaces. The challenges of incorporating so many requirements in a small area excited me. These challenges eventually inspired me! These were more like the Rubix cube you need to work and work to get it all right. And Practice makes a man perfect. Besides, you can't use up your creativity. The more you use, the more you have! That's the magic.

I started working independently and, there was no looking back. For me, success is not quantitative. The definition of success varies from person to person. If my designs are approved and executed and appreciated by my client, it's the happiness and satisfaction that is success for me. Of course, being paid aptly for the efforts is equally important. It adds to the zest and zeal.

I find doing interiors for residences more interesting and challenging. The interiors of commercial establishments are monotonous and mechanical. For residences, you need to interact with all the family members and get their likes/dislikes. You then whip them all in your designs, topping them with your own ideas, and come up with something that matches everyone's liking. In this process, the design evolved and tends to be different always. And different is always attractive!

This passion for interiors was accompanied by a passion for mirrors!! Yes, mirrors! I just didn't frame my mirrors but designed them. I gave them life. I can proudly claim that the mirrors, designed by me are totally unique. You can never find something like that anywhere! These objects of desire are totally out of the box kind. I more I developed them, the more creative I got. Can't help but praise myself a bit! It was like Creativity is Intelligence having fun!! It was not just about ideas, but about making ideas happen. I organized a couple of exhibitions as well in Hyderabad. I was approached by the Taj Group for my creations. That was a Real Achievement for me!

This journey of mine with mirrors was short-lived. Pregnancy and the joy of being a mother, the 2nd time, pushed all the other dreams backstage. It's been a long time, but I'm sure, my connection with mirrors is going to ignite pretty soon.

My journey with Interiors was perked by my involvement with the KSPCB. (Karnataka state pollution control board), as a Board member. This is more of a Social Responsibility. This came with new ideas...new thoughts. The focus is now. The Green Environment—eco-friendly and sustainable. Nearly pollution free. This post as a Board member, pushed me to new depths am seriously working on new initiatives, which will take time to materialize, but am sure of the results. At the magical age of 50, I dreamt of doing a certification course on green buildings, to become an Accredited Professional! I had quite a bit of studying to do. The saying..."Where there is a will, there's a way" is TRUE!!! This additional degree highlighting my name has now made me greedy for more! I now have a new list of courses to take up shortly. The best and the funny part is...I'm enjoying studying and taking up exams!

Architecture is frozen music, and the Interior is Flowing music! The first rule of decoration is that you can break almost all rules (Just that, you first need to master the rules, to break them). The best design trend is, not to follow one. In Interiors, creativity is a wild mind, with a disciplined eye. In my case, recollecting the mistakes that I committed as a beginner, it's good to be ...Flawed and Fabulous. Because perfect doesn't exist and Normal is boring.

The story of the next empty room is waiting to happen, and I'm the author! I wish the Homes and Abodes designed by me, inspire the inmates to go out into the world to do great things because life gets more beautiful with your Dreams coming true!

5

Giggles—Discovering Myself

Sunitha Kolar, Founder, Giggles

When I was asked to write about my start-up story, I realized there are so many droplets that have added to my journey. I was not even aware then. When I was 6 years old, I liked my nursery teacher. I wanted to please her. I offered to support her. She asked me to monitor the lower KG class for a few minutes whenever she had some work. I felt like the monster in the Onida advertisement (if you are born in the 80s you will understand). I loved being the leader, though it was for a few minutes they all had to listen to me. I felt very proud. I did not realize then that I loved doing that. When I was 12 years old, I loved taking care of my sister's children. I enjoyed feeding them, playing with them, and actually mothering them. Of Course, that was not considered as an interest or a skill set. I grew up with the belief that I have to study well so that I get a good job and get settled. I had no clue what passion is, what is following my heart, what are my interests, and what other possibilities I had. Nobody told me that we all have different skill sets and gifts that we can offer to the world.

It took me 15 years to realize my passion, possibilities and what I want to do with my life. I have been discovering my path, my life, my passion, and my strengths through various experiences like all of us.

Every incident, failure, wrong decision, interaction, and creation has helped me discover myself, layer by layer.

Before starting a business, I was just running like a mad chicken from one job to another. I was not happily working in any post or company. I mostly worked like a robot. The work did not make me feel alive. Once I started my business, I slowly started realizing my skills and strengths. The challenges of the start-up made me very much alive and flying high.

I started as a franchisee, started my own preschool, started a cathartic firm, and started an alternative learning space. So, it never stopped at one start-up. It has been evolving, changing, and transforming.

In the year 2017, I was standing in front of a paediatric clinic with my child and husband. A preschool bus was standing. Looking at the bus I said, "I wish I could start a preschool." After a week or two, my husband told me that his friend will invest if we start a preschool. He pushed me to start my journey as an entrepreneur. I don't think I would have started the business without his motivation. For me, business means I can do some work on my own, earn and still be a part of my child's development. My son was 1.6 years old then. So, it was important for me to be able to be there for him. My job did not allow me to have that.

As a child, I was labelled as a talkative person, too straightforward, too lazy, and so on. But some of those actually helped me. Being talkative helped me communicate and convince parents to enrol their children. When I was working in a company, I thought I was of no good, I thought I was a liability to the company. When I did something that I did not like. Obviously, I sucked at it. Everything that held me back then became the strengths that helped me move forward in my start-up. I started discovering that I am good at handling pressure, getting things done, negotiating, enrolling people, managing a team and being creative. Trust me, I had never even tried drawing scenery and here I was challenged to make puppets.

After I became a businesswoman, I have done things I had never done before. I have hammered posters, carried a ladder on my bike, done different kinds of artwork, spoken in front of huge crowds, built a rapport with police and other government officials, arranged funds in creative ways, rode on a scooter with big boxes of resources and much more. I could recognize all my hidden talents and skills when I was no longer an employee but my own boss. Doing something on my own has taught me more than what my school would teach. Until then I strongly believed that I was good for nothing.

In the initial days of the franchise, my husband and I woke up at four in the morning to put up posters in and around the area. Being in a business for the first time without any experience I didn't know what to do and how to do it. Because it was a franchise, I got some guidance from the company on how to start, how to talk to teachers, what would be the fee structure, what curriculum to follow, which toys to buy, how to make an appointment letter, etc and that helped to start the journey. Though there was guidance from the franchiser. There were still a lot of things to learn hands-on. Theoretical knowledge had to be put into action. In that process, I made a lot of mistakes and blunders. Slowly the learning happened on the go.

In the first year, I started with 17 children. As I found my new passion, I enjoyed running the business and being an entrepreneur. Slowly the business started picking up and we had more children joining us. On the professional front, I started gaining recognition and appreciation. Parents, children, and staff were very happy. I felt good that I had created this space for me and my child. As the preschool was only half-day, I had the rest of the day to spend with my child.

But personally, I was finding it hard to make ends meet and as my husband didn't have a stable income it was very challenging. I started taking up part-time jobs to get some money, selling books, and insurance and when nothing worked, I started using the income from the business for running the house. This started affecting the business and created financial dips to the point where I thought about selling my business.

I was expecting my second child. Along with pregnancy, there were other things that I had to manage. My marriage also was affected. I was mostly running the school alone. My parents were of huge support. Without their help, it would have been very difficult for me. The franchiser started pressuring me to increase the business. They wanted me to shift to a bigger building. Expand my space. I was struggling to manage monthly expenses both at school and at home. So, it was impossible for me to invest anymore and move to a bigger building. I could not handle the pressure. One day it affected my body and mind so much that I was not in my senses, I started screaming and crying "I don't want any business, I don't want anything, I don't want to deal with any of this." As it became unbearable, I thought it would be good for me to sell the business. I started looking for buyers. I almost sold my business to a couple. Due to the franchise intervention, the deal was cancelled. I was so shattered to the point that it provoked me to come out of the franchise and start my own business, Giggles Fun schooling. Though I hated that manager (who intervened), if I look back, I am actually very grateful to him. If he had not created problems, then I would have given up my passion and maybe joined some mundane job after delivery. And as I shared earlier, I did not enjoy working in some jobs. Yes, it was another gift in disguise. I am grateful to him; he is one of the reasons for my growth and for pushing me to pursue my passion.

Woohoo! Giggles started with a loss, or should I say debt? The good news was my best friend joined me as a partner. Yes, she is also crazy like me, she convinced her family to invest in a business which was under loss...just because she trusted me and the work we do.

The next year was a huge struggle, there were a lot of issues from the franchiser, debt to clear, broken marriage, visiting the police station(because of my husband), clearing the mess that my husband had created in his business, managing a new team, planning a new curriculum, maintaining the relationship with the school parents, managing housework, expenses, family and yes do you remember I had just delivered so nursing the child and how can you forget I had my son also who needed my attention. Should I make you feel like you are reading a script of a *ghisapita* (terrible) movie or a web series... here you go—I had to sell my gold jewellery to pay the school rent and salaries of the support staff. I did not make it as dramatic as it would be in a '90s movie. It was the best solution that I could think of. As there was no money to pay the teachers, I told them "I don't have money to pay you, girls, trust me I will clear it all, you might have to give me time. If anyone is not ok, I completely understand you can find another job as you will have your commitments" After such a vulnerable heart-melting sharing what do you expect? The teachers worked without salaries for six months. (Extra info: I made friends for life) Of course, I also had to work part-time to meet the school expenses and pay the salaries I had promised. Even without a brand name for the franchise, when school parents showed trust in me, it motivated me to take the risk and go on with Giggles. My friend joining me in this venture gave me strength in this tough time. Now we started marketing and building the brand of Giggles.

I remember in the initial years we were fighting to prove that Giggles is better than any other school. If we saw a new school board in the area, we would roll our eyes and say, "one more preschool." The fear of surviving among the many preschools in the area was constantly there. We tried to be on par with them and we visited different preschools to make sure we weren't lagging in the race. We did marketing by putting up posters, banners, and flyers. We did everything possible to make our presence stand out from the other preschools in the area.

We realized that all these decisions came from fear, fear of not being successful or fear of failing. That was a stressful space to run the show. Slowly we shifted our focus from fear to love, fear of failure to love for the work, love for children, and love for making a difference. Then we saw without much effort, Giggles started standing out. We stopped worrying about what other schools had to offer that we don't have, how big their building was and what new toys they had. We started to focus on what we love to do, create, and offer. We were no longer worried about new schools emerging around us. We were enjoying creating moments and memories every day in Giggles.

In 2014, I started open schooling for my two children. To understand and build conviction in the concept, I started visiting alternative learning spaces. In this journey, I learnt a lot. I got a whole new level of understanding about a child's learning capabilities. I got introduced to a new concept called self-directed learning. With these discoveries, my approach changed from teaching to facilitating. That made a big impact on the learning at Giggles. Giggles started evolving from a rigid preschool to an open learning space, not just for the children, but for the parents, grandparents and all the members of Giggles. To bring the community together, we created different opportunities through events and gatherings. We did events like circle fest- street painting, family day, grandparents' day, a mural workshop for parents, and installation of Ganesh to name a few. Circle fest was the biggest event I have ever organized. With a lot of effort, we got permission to paint the street. So, we invited the Giggles community and everyone in the neighbourhood to paint circles on the road. This event got us recognition and admissions.

Looking back at my experience, I'm very happy to see how with no experience in business or teaching, I took up a franchise, started my preschool and converted it into a community of learners. Being a woman and being an entrepreneur isn't a cakewalk. When we are passionate about something and trying to create that in the world, many distractions come in the form of breakdowns. The reason that I'm sharing my personal experiences vulnerably is to share that we all have our personal struggles which keep pulling us down. I want to say that we don't have to give up on our passion or dreams because of these passing clouds. These experiences are only making us creative in handling situations.

Talking about challenging experiences… The next challenge in my life was going through my divorce. Being a single parent of two children, and the only child to my parents it was scary to take this step. But it was necessary. If you want to know more about my date with the judge or my adventures of single parenting you can mail me, I have some fun stories to share.

Though it was very scary to restart my life at 35...it was reassuring to know that I have a community to support. I got a lot of support. I could sail through this tough time with the help of my parents, children, friends, and my new family Giggles.

It's important for all of us to create a non-judgmental, loving, and caring community around us because we are all interdependent creatures and life becomes simpler when you have people around you that lift you and support you or just say 'I Love you and I am with you.' I was lucky to have that in my life.

Giggles evolving was a constant process. We have been able to grow because we have been open to learning. To keep enhancing the learning space, I brought different topics and resources to the team. I brought different people to host sessions on topics like multiple intelligence, handicrafts, painting, music and movements, dance, creating a vision, reflection, using different teaching aids, etc. That helped each and every person in the team discover their potential. As and when each team member started discovering strengths and passion that reflected in their work. That was seen in the development of the children and the loyalty of the parent community.

The community was getting bigger, we had various activities like preschool, daycare, math, art, language classes and so on. We at giggles are a crazy team. We loved doing things *hatke* (different) and going against the stereotype. So, in 2020, we decided to not torture children to practice and perform on the normal annual day. Instead, we came up with the concept of family day where families of all the children, parents, grandparents, uncles, and aunts came together to spend a day. After Family Day, the plan was to involve the whole family in the learning of the child, shifting the focus from child-oriented to involving the whole family in the child's learning process. We had cleaned the ground opposite with the idea of inviting more people into the community. We had different plans for expanding giggles to the next level.

When the lockdown first started, we thought it would only last for a week or two. We decided to make use of the situation to sterilize the space and the resources. We were preparing for the summer camp and the upcoming academic year. We had no idea of closing the business. But when covid hit us, we had to decide to close down the business. Because of the uncertainty, it was very difficult to continue any further. Though my friend and I thought that this was the best thing to do at this time, it was the toughest decision that we ever had to make. We sold all the toys; we gave away a few things and we took some support from some parents to store resources with the hope of starting again one day.

After waiting for 3 months, we felt closing the space was the wise option. In June 2020, we decided to close Giggles Fun schooling. When we announced the closure of Giggles, we were showered with love and concern from the community. We were supported by school parents, the staff, and the owner. They supported us emotionally, financially, and by being present physically even in times of covid.

Then came the day when we had to hand over the building to the owner. My friend and I sat down in one of the rooms, we held hands and thanked each and every person who supported us on this journey. We thanked the building for contributing so much. We thanked all the children, the team and all the parents for being with us to date. We thanked the universe for always having our back. We took a few minutes to pour out all our emotions which we were holding back until then.

After the closure of Giggles, staying at home was very difficult for me. Apart from the delivery of my child, I have never ever stayed at home for so long. I've always been a people person and when there was no Giggles, no children, and no interacting with the parents it impacted me hugely. I was very depressed. It took a while for me to find my new balance and a new routine. The emotions kept coming back every now and then. I had to often pull myself out of sadness and low phase. With the help of my friends, family, and mentors, I gathered the courage which was shaken up last year and started the pilot project, Discover Me, an open learning space. A new challenge for me was to reinvent and rediscover myself for my new journey.

Discover Me was started as a pilot project—a summer camp for three weeks in April 2021. I have always dreamt of having an alternative learning space. We had children from 2yrs to 15 years coming to the camp. I wanted to create a space that curates experiences for every child, every individual that helps them to learn, grow and discover their learning style, their potential, strengths, and weaknesses.

While offering space for others the bonus was, I discovered myself. I discovered my potential and passion further. It rebuilt my confidence that I am capable of running an open learning centre. Being at home for more than a year made me doubt myself. You see we all have this addiction to self-judgment. We keep underestimating ourselves and judging everything we do. When I pushed myself to start "Discover Me" (I had a butterfly in my stomach). One of the children asked, "15 years ago you have already started a business so it should not be difficult for you this time right?" I bit my tongue and thanked that child for teaching me to have trust in myself. When I am stuck in life, I have many such junior consultants and counsellors.

I don't know whether this is the end of the story of my start-up because I don't know what life has in store for me. I am ready for all the adventure life has to offer me. As you see in my story, change is one thing that is constant.

The mantra that helps me to thrive in life is—

All of life comes to me with ease and joy.

Trust the process of life and enjoy the ride.

6

Connecting the Dots

Srividya Puppala, Founder and CEO,

Ensconce Business Process Consulting Services LLP

This Story is a tribute to my younger sister Late Ms Mamta Puppala who herself has been an inspiration to many professionals in the Healthcare industry via her research, publications, and software development in the AI space at Houston Methodist USA, one of the reputed institutions for medicine and research.

Our Company had the honour of getting featured as Iconic Brand of 2022 this August 2022 by Blossoms Media in association with Bombay Stock Exchange SME, featured this January 2022 in the Hall of Fame Edition of Enterprise World Magazine, received Atmanirbhar Bharat Award 2021 for Business Consulting, and also being featured in one of the prestigious New York-based Magazine CIO Views. It was a proud moment for me, my family, and my team. While I have experienced many such memorable moments, life threw at me some tough situations and challenges too. As the saying goes "When the going gets tough, the tough get going." In my case, my family played a vital role in ensuring that I remain tough and that my core is not shaken, no matter how hard the situation/challenge is.

I was born into a middle-class family and grew up in *Bhilai* (a part of the Hindi heartland) with my roots in Srikakulam and Chittoor. My father, Mohan Rao, a retired Deputy Manager of the Bhilai Refractories Plant, and my Mother Santha Kumari, a retired Bank officer, a Lawyer, and extremely enterprising women were my biggest source of inspiration. My better half Girish Gadamsetty who heads the Business Operations at Adobe Systems has been a pillar of support throughout, especially during my entrepreneurial journey.

During my early childhood years, my first love was Music. I thoroughly cherished those 12 years of learning Carnatic Classical from my Guru, Mrs Hema Vishwanathan. I have learned the best part of music, viz, playing with *Swaras* and getting creative with *Gamakas*; It is magical to create connections between the musical notes. Music binds you with your inner self and brings out the best in you. *Puppala Sisters* (me and my sister) as we were called, rocked the stage for six years back-to-back in a row in Lata Mangeshkar competitions held at Bhilai Nagar.

For building my foundation strong during my schooling years, my sincere appreciation to Mr PK Nair, Mr Rastogi, and Mr Chandwani. I got a really good score at PET Entrance and secured free seats in RECs (now NIT) in Indore, Gwalior, and Bhopal. I was pretty excited to study at REC Engineering College, but my destiny had different plans. I had to move to southern India with my parents. I joined SRM Easwari Engineering College, Chennai to pursue my Bachelor's in Computer Science and Engineering. I topped Madras University in Engineering Drawing in my first year. I owe Mrs Maragatham, our Computer Science Professor, and Mr Rajendran, our HOD for supporting me in the next steps of my higher education.

The last leg of my formal education took me to the United States of America where I completed my Master's in Electrical and Computer Engineering from the University of Massachusetts (UMass), Lowell. I was one of the very few students in the University to be chosen for the Software Developer position at UMass Lowell. It was a great opportunity for me as I could develop my hands-on Software Skills and more importantly experience a professional work environment for the first time.

I developed my software engineering expertise in the USA working with companies in the Education Sector, eCommerce Segment, Atmospheric Sciences, and Telecom segment. One of my best experiences was with ANPI, Springfield, Illinois, USA, and I owe a lot to Mr Jeff Wheaton for believing in me all along. I developed my skill in application development from legacy programming languages to .NET and attained Microsoft Certification as Certified Professional in .NET.

After having worked in the USA for about 5 years, I and my husband decided to move back to India for good in 2005 to be with our ageing parents. On our return to India, I joined Tata Consultancy Services in 2005 as a Technical Lead where I managed the development of twenty Odd Applications and eCommerce projects for Microsoft. I got certified in SQL Server and also as Microsoft Architect. TCS, one of the best consulting companies in the Software space recognized my calibre and invested in my growth. I was chosen to be one of the first twelve employees of TCS India to get Certified as a PROPELler to conduct PROPEL Confluences for Professional Excellence, Role Enhancement, Empowerment and Ownership Culture.

A significant milestone in my personal life is becoming a mother. With the immense support of my in-laws and parents, I survived those demanding years balancing both home and work. My child's health forced me to move to Hyderabad and I had to switch jobs.

I joined Infosys as one of the youngest Project Managers. Infosys' experience was enterprising. I managed multiple accounts for end-to-end Project/Program/Account Management and Delivery. Apart from my core Technical and Managerial responsibilities, I always enjoyed taking on additional responsibilities like Quality Auditing, People, and Talent Development. I also managed fourteen different verticals in the Retail Segment across domains for Reuse, Process, and Quality Compliance.

It so happened that during my maternity break, one of the IIMB Alumni running his start-up approached me through LinkedIn and sought my help in setting up the business and certain management processes for the company for business development. Little did I know that experience can be a trigger point to provide management and establishment services for such start-ups and mid-aged companies.

After my parenting break, I then worked for Fidelity Investments where I contributed as Development Manager bringing in process improvements, and best practices for software automation projects. My last experience before instituting ENSCONCE was with UST Global. I was hired as a Portfolio Development Manager for one of their customers, a global leader in the retail pharmacy and wellness segment, I managed their multiple Programs and Portfolios. I thoroughly enjoyed the experience of managing the show for this global leader. I also contributed to the internal Centre of Excellence Practice at UST Global, developing the best practices and talent at UST Global.

Throughout my corporate career, I had the opportunity to independently handle multiple functions, large teams, and stakeholders in different sectors like Lifesciences, Healthcare, Entergy Utilities, Financial, Retail, and Education—for companies from Europe and US regions. I managed Portfolio Development, COE, Global Delivery, Account Governance, Process Control & Quality Compliance. I had gathered vital experience in eCommerce, Advanced Technologies & Integration Technologies space.

My corporate work experience has strengthened my ability to manage multiple time-bound projects with a Quality mindset, leverage People and Process enablers, Empower People with Opportunities, manage end-to-end Customer Delivery, and build great Customer Experience and Customer Governance Factors.

The biggest disruption to my professional life was triggered by the thought of creating my own company. Although this became a reality in 2017, the seeds of which were sown in 2011 albeit accidentally, when

I helped the Consulting company to set up its internal business frameworks. As I reflected and introspected further, I noticed that I had been into Organizational development, People Empowerment, Quality, and Process Compliance since 2006 for 13 long years. These are the demands of growing Businesses too. Having seen the IT industry grow immensely by leveraging mature tools and processes, I strongly believed that small and mid-size Businesses could also benefit significantly by leveraging the IT industry's process knowledge.

And with that vision, ENSCONCE came into existence. ENSCONCE means "to establish or settle (someone) in a comfortable, safe place." I Instituted ENSCONCE (*www.ensconce.in*) with the passion of bringing my expertise and bridging the gaps in the areas of Organizational Development, Organizational Culture, People-Process Enablement, and Business Growth.

I spent the next few months defining the vision for my organization. I reached out to several entrepreneurs who were kind enough to share their challenges, learnings, and knowledge. I absorbed all their wisdom like a thirsty dry sponge when dropped in water. I owe my family and friends for supporting me in and out when we had tough times during those initial years. I owe a lot to my mentors, Mr M R Ramaswamy and Mr Bharat Ravuri whose inputs were and continue to be invaluable to my company's growth.

As we started interacting and working with several traditional Small and Mid-size organizations, we noticed a common pattern across most of them… they failed to recognize the importance of proactively investing in process and culture early on in their journey. The alarm bell starts ringing when they are unable to sustain or achieve the desired pace of growth. The change to recovery from this phase is possible but their precious time is lost in the recovery process. This is a vicious cycle and many MSMEs fall into the trap of non-performance.

We adopted a multi-prong strategy to increase the stickiness among these businesses about the importance of leveraging mature business processes to achieve sustainable long-term growth:

- Spread awareness and educate small & mid-size Businesses through various online & offline programs, and conferences on the importance of business processes.
- Partner with MSME Development Institute, Bangalore, Government of India. Thanks to Mrs Suman S. Raju, MSME asst. Director, MSME-DI Bangalore for sharing the vision and giving us the opportunity for the Development of Small and Mid-Size Businesses.
- Partner with Universities and Educational institutions. There is a famous Chichewa proverb that says, "M'mera mpoyamba" literally translated as "catch them while young."

The journey of ENSCONCE was never easy. As a brand-new start-up, with no mindshare, it was quite challenging to create a footfall... especially when my network is limited to just corporate professionals. Trust is a very important factor for any organization. I am highly indebted to our first set of customers and partners who believed in us for our Services.

When the pandemic impacted our core business, we continued to remain invested in our existing customers but more importantly, we were quick enough to anticipate and expand our offerings and achieve growth through diversification. We continued to have healthy top and bottom-line growth, and our teams and partners didn't have to take any pay cuts or undergo job loss which has also been a huge satisfaction to us.

ENSCONCE is best known for Offering Services—Business & HR Transformation, Recruitment, outsourced HR functions, Statutory/ Factory Audits & Compliances, Corporate Training & Training Events, Employee & Customer Engagement activities, Branding & Marketing Services. I joined hands in 2021 with one of the multimillion-dollar companies STS Worldwide, USA, providing Growth Advisory, Funding, Mergers, and Acquisitions. This has further fuelled my aspiration to bring change in MSMEs & fuel growth opportunities in this segment further. I believe that the strength of building strong and enduring brands is through an amalgamation of people, processes, technology, quality, innovation, and continuous improvement.

Dr APJ Abdul Kalam once said, *"You have to dream before your dreams can come true"*.

My journey has been phenomenal and very satisfying.

7

The Unstoppable

Namrata Agarwal, Founder, Vishisht Lifestyle

Hi, I am Namrata Agarwal, founder of Vishisht Lifestyle, an eco-friendly brand offering natural skin care products. On a mission to support our planet, I focus on improving the skincare space by offering all-natural products delivered in zero-waste packaging. Like any other start-up entrepreneur, I wear many hats throughout the day to run my small business. I handle marketing, customer support, social media and sometimes even photo shoots.

Before starting my business, I worked in a Multinational Accounting firm as an Auditor for 4.5 years and, I am a Certified Public Accountant. I got selected for the job during college placement programmes. I liked my job and learnt a lot during my tenure there. I developed both personal and professional skills and got groomed from a college kid to a working professional. The pay was great. I liked what I do. I had a good lifestyle with so many friends as colleagues. However, I always had a feeling inside me that I want to start something of my own. Although a fixed job offers stability and security, I wanted to be my boss, work on my terms, and take vacations on my terms.

As I wondered what I could create, I developed rashes on my skin one summer. I tried different moisturizer brands, but none of them helped. I researched online and learned about the harmful chemicals found in mass-produced skincare products. These chemicals cause damage to our skin in the long term and, they are also bad for our planet. I read some blogs and subscribed to newsletters of skin doctors & Ayurveda specialists.

I learnt about natural alternatives such as pure coconut oils, Shea butter, essential oils etc. These alternatives have skin benefits, and they are kind to our planet. Soon, I started formulating recipes using these natural ingredients. I prepared moisturizers, scrubs, lip balms, hair serums etc. I tried them myself and gave family and friends to try. To my surprise, these homemade products worked well. My skin rashes went and never came back. I decided I will never buy products filled with nasty chemicals any longer and, I will create my natural skincare products at home. Since I got a great response from family and friends with their experience of my homemade products, I felt that this is what I want to pursue. I got an incredible amount of support from my family and friends. They encouraged me to leap.

I had no idea of how to run a business or where to start. I Googled everything from finding suppliers to booking a domain. I used to work on my research and my start-up idea during weekends and worked full-time at my job Monday to Friday. It took six months to finalize the list of products to launch, find the suppliers for my raw materials, trial & error for the formulation, register my business, get a GST certificate etc. I finally reached a point where it became impossible to work full-time and work on my start-up at the same time. With a heavy heart, I finally quit my job. The feeling was scary because my monthly paycheck stopped coming and, my business was nowhere close to launching. I became very conscious of my spending and used my life savings for my start-up capital. The next couple of months went into designing the website, designing the labels, photoshoots etc. This period took up a lot of patience because things were not moving too fast and delayed the website launch. I was not willing to give up and kept reminding myself why I started all this in the first place. We finally launched in May 2018.

The last few years have been quite a journey. Entrepreneurship teaches so many lessons—to be vulnerable, to be fearless, to deal with embarrassment, to deal with an empty bank account and most of all—to never give up. During our journey, we all make mistakes—big or small but we always figure things out. That is the beauty of entrepreneurship. I run a small business. I may not have a fancy lifestyle but, I wouldn`t want it any other way. I feel truly blessed and grateful that I am living my dream life, I am doing what I love, and I am following my purpose.

I am passionate about leading a sustainable lifestyle and incorporating those practices in my business as well. My brand Vishisht is on a mission to divert tons of plastic ending up in landfills and oceans by offering sustainable skincare alternatives. All the products are packed and delivered in minimal, low waste and plastic-free packaging. The materials used in the final packaging include glass jars, product labels, paper wrap, fillers, corrugated boxes, and tape. They are reusable, recyclable and, some are even compostable. There is a jar return policy where customers can send back their used jars once they have collected 4 of them. To motivate them, we offer exclusive discounts in exchange for returned jars. This practice helps promote a circular economy by closing the loop and using what we already have.

Vishisht avoids excess consumerism by offering a limited range of multi-purpose products made using minimum materials to ensure people only buy what they need rather than spoiling them for choices. As a brand, we are conscious of every step right from production to final delivery. During the entire process, we work with minimum materials, reuse & recycle every material and work in natural light to the extent possible to conserve energy. We are carbon-neutral and offset 100% of our CO2 emissions generated from delivering packages by contributing to green projects.

With our continuous efforts, we have diverted more than 50,000 grams of plastic from oceans and landfills. We have offset more than

4,040 Kgs of CO2 equivalent to saving 353 trees and powering 401 light bulbs.

Sustainability and ethical practices remain at the core of our business. For us, the planet & people come before profit. The products are prepared in small batches using fresh ingredients every month and have never been tested on animals.

Through Vishisht, I wish to encourage more people to choose a sustainable lifestyle and switch to eco-friendly products. Small changes such as switching to a bamboo toothbrush, using cloth bags for grocery shopping, using steel or copper bottles, carrying own cutlery, ditching single-use plastic etc., can also be a great benefit to our planet. We don`t need a few people to do things perfectly. Instead, we need a lot of people to do these things imperfectly. Every single effort counts. We have come this far and still have a long way to go. I am excited about this journey and can`t wait to see what the future holds.

8

UMBARA—Women Crossing Threshold

Rama Narayanan
Umbara Designs

"Empathy is the engine that powers all the best in us. It is what civilises us. It is what connects us"

—Meryl Streep

When I was growing up, there was always a handmade activity. Almost every little thing around the house from utility items were made aesthetically. Looking back, working with my hands is what sustained me through difficult times.

I was 12 years of age when mom bought in the teal blue sewing machine second hand from an aged person in the early 80's. The machine was smooth and showed a lot of love and care from the previous owner. Amma was the mother of three fast paced girls growing into their teens. Amma always kept us well dressed and well presented, and she decided to sew us the clothes we would be needing as we grew. Newly diagnosed with diabetes, amma developed calf pain when she pedalled. So, we became a team, I would sit in front of the machine, and she would sit at the machine. While her hands would guide the seam, I would pedal. On hindsight, I reverse pedalled. And that is where my journey started. By the time, I graduated I had a thriving business making money from designing and tailoring clothes for friends and neighbours. I used to take tuitions for students a few years below my age. Little did I know that teaching and sewing would come together to form UMBARA.

Making things, became second nature and I qualified professionally in handmade and machine-made designer clothing. Working in the industry for 17 long years, somehow, the corporate culture and the regimental treatment to the hands that made the clothes left me with a distaste. Heavily masculinised, the system was wilting and drying personally and didn't appeal to my design sensibilities.

Making money is one thing, losing one's soul is another. I turned around to a complex world of commoditisation of everyday life. Things were gaining traction and priority in social living and were quickly becoming denominators for evaluating success. But life styles were being built on soulless things.

It was right about this time that I discovered my ability to read non-verbal training and hand eye coordination skills and their impact on new neural pathways. No, I didn't get a PhD. All my learning have come from life lessons. I learnt the skill from taking care of a person affected by stroke and while training a few women to work with their hands.

I chose to quit the industrialised clothing line, to nurse a bed ridden person at home. This decision was the turning point and defined the quality with which UMBARA would be designed as a business. The doctor told us, there are two ways to open up blocked neural pathways in a stroke patient. One, through their will power slowly movements will come back. Two, by repetitive movements, the limbs work new ways to connect to the brain. It took us over two years to get her to bring back basic motions into her control. A very different style of functioning flowered in her, and her personality changed from who she was before the stroke. I understood that years of practice that our educational system puts us through works similarly. It is not all brain, but also the most infantile cognitive ability to learn hand and eye coordination, which we do from when we are a baby.

The women came in from varied backgrounds having various challenges, be they financial, physical, psychological, emotional. Society has no dearth if fall outs by adopting its systems of madness and money economy. I received many too. I realised the science and the skill set alone will not be enough. I took the help of a psychologist to support the stories of pain. I worked steadily on breaking up the task of making future products into edible bits of activities that the women could engage in. We started from rangoli at the threshold, to segregating bits of rags and counting buttons. Embroidery was the first evolving interest. Machines often represent a fearsome aspect of embracing their own power. So it takes the women in training anywhere between 3-6 month sometimes a year for them to make a breakthrough. The fun part for me was designing tasks and activities that helped each woman tide over her own gaping wide thresholds. Threshold to acceptance, acknowledgement, strength and many more. The financial burden of sustaining the women through training was supported by my personal funds and family support. UMBARA took roughly three years to earn its own keep. Once, products taking form, it became easier to show the Community what was possible. We adopt a method of each one teach one in the organisation.

There is no place for hierarchy, and we have a transparent flat system of communication. The women today learn remotely, and we have three small groups of women skilled in the line of sewn goods, raised singly by a woman who came to us for her own sustenance.

Society has a culture of utilising resources without giving back. I kind of rape culture. Not enough is done to develop potential and work with possibilities. Vocational training is now abandoned to NGOs. We traverse a wide barren phase where all that can be exploited is being taken. A sense of abundance is very hard for individuals to experience and hold. UMBARA is a small symbol of bringing back the possibility of life to barrenness.

Suffice to say, a huge urge within me rose to cognise a solution to the pain that I had experiencing . I created UMBARA—the threshold. Piece by piece, assimilating tools, methods, systems, techniques all the while training women from unemployable backgrounds, a solution through handwork creating new ways of looking at their life challenges.

Evan Charmicheal says, let your pain be the purpose. I did. More than 200 woman who seek dignity and strength to shoulder their personal journeys have walked through the threshold of UMBARA.

UMBARA creates conscious clothing, a bit of soul work in every unit. It is no surprise that our clients often say, bad day, good day, auspicious day our clothing are sought out of the melange of clothes in the cupboard.

Eco friendly, zero waste, social viable manufacturing, and consistent with fit, flair and choices.

Slow fashion is not just a green washing word for us. Our system follows the kanban system of manufacturing, and just in time deliveries thus minimising costs. Our women are technically sound and conversant in fabric, drape, fall, fit, construction, ease of movement; terms that many a qualified fashion designers dread to write on their resume.

9

Dream to Reality—Silence to Success

Chitra Balasubramaniam

Founder, SHEpreneurs Academy

Here's a story of a mum who has been through the boat of being a stay-at-home individual and later took charge to change her life to be everything she dreamt of being in life. The story is not just about being in both spaces of working or staying at home vs outside the home.

It is also a quest of hers to break the myths designed by society. Also, her story gives insight into understanding winning situations, like a complete introvert becoming an image consultant turned entrepreneur, author, podcaster, business strategist, forex trader and an investor.

A story where one doesn't want that sheltered cocoon and instead dares to dream ahead. "I was born in Chennai in a very conservative middle-class family. Growing up I saw my parents, especially my mother work hard as a government employee and I was determined to chart a different course for my career. My parents had a typical mindset and were keen that I study well, get a job, and marry a well-settled man. But from a young age, I was determined I would be an entrepreneur. I was very clear that I would not settle in a typical 9–5 job and would spend the maximum time with my kids as they grow.

Likewise, I was slowly fascinated by the entrepreneurial spirit and was always attracted to the people who were successful in their lives. I aspired to travel and, after finishing school I proudly announced my intentions to join air hostess training. My mother was completely against this as she believed that if I became so independent, I would refuse to marry. So, keeping my dreams aside, I continued with my college degree, just to satisfy them.

My parents were also very strict, and I was never allowed to go out with friends, no friends allowed in the house either, or never allowed to talk to strangers, especially men. Over time, I became a complete introvert and was never comfortable or confident talking to people.

Once I finished college, my parents started looking for a match for me. At that time, I saw marriage as a route to freedom and hastily said yes because I believed that I would be able to pursue my interests after marriage. While I was trying to adjust to my new life, I got pregnant with the first child and instantly got swept into the world of motherhood.

Life continued to throw hurdles my way in the form of family issues, failed business, and a debt of over 2 crores. Ten years passed and we were just trying to meet the ends. We cleared all the debts by then and got comfortable. It's not an easy task to come out of debt unlike getting into one. At the end of the day everything is about ATTITUDE, your choices, and the way you respond to situations speak about your attitude. As parents we always work as a team, we never stopped smiling or letting others or our kids know what we are going through, we always kept our sanity, and we did everything and anything to get an extra penny, as long as it's ethical & legal we did the business. We got into the transport business, auto, real estate, and anything you can think of, we did it till we cleared every penny of debt. Clearly, it's not easy as it sounds but it's worth the journey as we learned from every situation. But what happens when you get comfortable? I conceived my second son and soon got busy with him. But I also began to feel a void within myself.

I felt something was missing and life became monotonous where all I did was get up, cook, clean, feed kids & husband, make them comfortable, feed them again, sleep and repeat the same thing day in and day out. It was really frustrating sometimes. There was no outlet, no friends and being an introvert, I never went out or explored things alone.

Suddenly one day you realize that being comfortable is so fatal, you don't even notice when it's killing your dreams, and that day, I made a decision that I must make a choice to take a chance, or my life will never change—I will remain the same person whom I hated to be in the future.

Of course, I had fears, fear of having friends, talking to strangers, doing something on my own, and getting out of my comfort zone. But I made a decision to work on my fears and change.

Soon life around me began to change and great things started to happen when I came out of my comfort zone.

You are never too old to set another goal or to dream a new dream. This has been my mantra from early on, even though I have been an introvert all my life. I knew if I want to change my future, I need to change myself instead of the situations which are never going to happen.

I pushed myself to join courses in image consulting, makeup, soft skills, and etiquette, where I thoroughly enjoyed learning, meeting new people, and going out with friends. It was like new life, I started feeling young again and I became friends with younger people which made me feel younger and happier.

Of course, being an entrepreneur is not easy. If it was as easy as a breeze everyone would be an entrepreneur and be successful. Fortunately and unfortunately, that's not the case; it takes decisions, work ethic, commitment, discipline, planning, taking risks, a good team and last but not least, never giving up on your dreams. You have to keep reminding yourself that being an entrepreneur is delayed gratification. Today, when my older son is 26 years old and younger one is 16 years old and most women give up on their dreams, I want to say that my life is just beginning. Being a mother is an incredible journey as such, every mom would agree to that. As a mom, I have not given life to them, but they have given life to me. I don't want to look back on my life and realize that I wasted the precious time I had with my children by living in a state of perpetual distractions.

I wanted my children to see that their mom has had the courage to dream big and see me as their inspiration, someone who has not been afraid and is following her dreams irrespective of her age or situation. I speak to them openly about my venture and what kind of work I do, and how much time and energy I have to invest to follow my dreams. When you talk openly to your spouse and children, they do understand how badly you want to fulfil your dream. They support you. Successful mothers are not the ones that have never struggled, they are the ones that never give up despite the struggles.

Today I am in the crux of my life where I transform many people's lives through my journey and my experience, I run 4 successful companies, authored 3 best sellers, making passive income as an investor and couple of other businesses. Life is fulfilling personally and professionally. The only advice I would give anyone who wants success in life is to never quit and it's never too late to start any journey to success. It's all about the dream, work ethic and commitment you make that dream a reality.

Never let excuses get in the way of your success. My excuses were "I am an introvert, it's too late to start now, imposter syndrome, societal norms, what others might think" etc etc, but when I smashed through all the excuses, my path become very clear and effortless. The dream become a reality, from silence to success.

10

Young Versatility at its Best

Chitra Lele, Founder, Chitra Lele & Associates

When I started out my corporate journey three years ago in the hard-core corporate IT settings, I had this impression that through the corporate world, I could contribute to the greater good of the world. But as days went by, in the initial month of the employee induction itself, being a spirituality-driven person, I could immediately sense the undercurrent of corrupt business practices and team processes. Thereafter, the Spirit Techpreneur or Enlightened Engineer (one who blends the limitless dynamics of spirituality with the limited principles of technology to develop solutions for the collective community) within me sprang into action. I came up with my own manifesto for a new (basically a corruption-free) business ecosystem for the company that I got placed in. I knew to bring about transformative changes, buy-in from the higher-ups is necessary, but I failed to spot the hidden component of this equation: the higher-ups themselves did not want to change the faulty setup as it was introduced by them for serving their own agendas.

After I presented my manifesto to the higher-ups, I was slowly and steadily harassed for standing up against corruption and for standing firmly rooted in my truth in terms of integrity and honesty. Thereafter, the next six months were harrowing as hell for me, as everyone turned against me for speaking the truth. That is when I realized that to bring about positive progress, at times, one has to step out of the corrupt system and try and change it through the outside-in approach by setting a shining example. My two strongest pillars of support, my parents, Asha Lele and G. G. Lele, supported my decision of stepping out of this maze of corporate mess and making that much-needed move towards starting my own venture. Right from day one, we have been designing SpiritTech solutions based on the paradigm of Ethically Aligned Design (EAD) principles where trust and transparency are of paramount importance. And that is how my own software firm Chitra Lele and Associates came into existence, and thereafter my passion project Chitra Cares was also launched.

Through my ventures, I want to contribute to the collective community and the greater good of our world. Hence, we design systems that are in line with Ethically Aligned Design principles. Rather than merely focusing on developing software applications that make everyone dependent on the matrix of information revolution and control, we tend to focus our efforts on developing socially and morally responsible applications that will help one and all to draw their gaze inwards.

At the organizational level (or for that matter in all spheres of life), ethical leadership is about introducing spirituality at work/sphere. This requires leaders who have activated their inner leader to help establish a culture based on transformative mission statements and progressive business practices that promote personal well-being as well as team growth. Spirituality-driven, ethical leadership focuses more on responsibilities rather than rights. And this is the new initiative that I am working on.

Recently, in 2020, I was recognized for my revolutionary work in the field of Information Technology, both as a tech author and young mentor by the reputed online mentoring hub: IndiaMentor. Through my technology-related books, I share my novel approaches and enhanced ecosystems to bring about positive progress in corporate settings. All my work, be it ongoing research studies, software projects, peace policies, academic books, or spirituality seminars, have one central theme—helping individuals, teams and organizations ignite their inner spark.

Apart from progressing in my computer science field, I want to contribute to society through the fields of literature, education and peace-making. To encourage all, especially young people of my age, to join the bandwagon of peace-making and social transformation is my life purpose. Through my on-the-field campaigns, software projects, academic books, spirituality seminars and my association with peace organizations, I started living out my purpose from a young age, since the year 2017. I am only at the first step of my journey and have a long way to go!

Meet the Co-Authors

Aanika Gajendragad

Aanika is a 15-year-old homeschooler who left school to focus on her career as a writer. She's been writing since the age of 9 and making a career out of it seemed like the best option. She left school in 2021 as she didn't want to focus on the subjects she didn't like—maths and science. She has featured in a few anthologies and also has a website she writes blogs in, muchbyaanika.com.

Reggie Menacherry

Reggie Menacherry is a photographer, mural painter, comic artist, certified yoga trainer, home chef, failed comedian, published author in a travel anthology book, and passionate about contributing to society. He is a corporate enslaved person, but a case of a gentleman who went rogue to travel with his tent and camera, taking three years of sabbatical from work-life; living in the jungles, snowy mountains, farming communities, and working in small cafes. All this while living & experiencing different shades of life, weaving stories, and now learning to write a few.

Nilkesh Sonawane

Based in Navi Mumbai, Maharashtra, Nilkesh is a Hotelier by profession and Writer by Heart. He finds his passion in writing. His best card in play is 'Suspense'. He Says, "Not only Horror and Thriller, But also in Fantasy, Adventure, Romance, or even Comedy! Suspense is an Important key for a story, without it, any story is incomplete!"

Nilkesh is also passionate about Visual Storytelling. He finds Cinema as the best tool to immerse your audience into your world of stories! He has started his baby steps into the industry by making a handful of Short-Films. "Whether I get the recognition or not, I will keep Writing Stories. Till my last breath!" He adds.

Kali Sitholey Rawat

Kali Rawat is an author who dons many hats. A Professor of fashion design, a mother and new author, her work is an evocative take on the realities and unrealities of life. She has previously published a book of short stories called "The Well and Other Stories", in addition to several research papers on varied topics ranging from fashion to feminism. Kali lives in Mumbai, India with her family but dreams of retiring to the Himalayas and writing full time in front of a roaring fire as the snow swirls outside her windows.

Sandhita Agarwal

Sandhita is a software developer by profession but a hippie at heart. She likes to travel the world and meet different people. She completed her Masters in AI and ML from LJMU, UK. She is one of the authors showcased in the anthology Minds@Work2, Quarantine Tales, and Love Unvoiced. When not writing or coding, she can be found listening to true crime documentaries and reading up on conspiracies. She lives with her spunky cocker spaniel in Bangalore and hopes to have a tête-à-tête with Salman Rushdie one day.

Tejase Rathod

Tejase Rathod is an aspiring doctor. She enjoys gaming as a way to escape reality, and writes to refresh her mind. She loves cats and eyeliners and believes in finding joy in the little things in life.

Vaishnavi Tawade

Vaishnavi is an aspiring Counseling Psychologist based in Mumbai, India. Apart from her interest in psychology, she also enjoys reading and writing. She has a flair for art and is also a food enthusiast. As an inquisitive person that she is, she loves to seek new experiences. Vaishnavi ardently believes that the world can be a better place if we show love, kindness and empathy towards ourselves and each other.

Shaymi Shah

Shaymi Shah is a creative content writer by passion. Most of her writing comes from observations of everyday life. Today, through a lot of practice, she has successfully imbibed in herself the skill of weaving stories—stories one can easily lose themselves in. Apart from her debut book of poems, she has written short stories and poems for over 40 anthologies. She is currently establishing her brand of lifestyle products and corporate gifts called SOEL.

Halo Golwin

Halo Golwin is not merely a symbol, but an epithet for Golwin's whimsical friend who inspired him to exercise personal freedom through writing. With the might of the pen, Golwin's work often brings out the absurd in the mundane and uses humour to amplify the insane. If you are an avid lover of poetry and art, give him a visit at @not_a_blank_slate_anymore on Instagram!

Mridini Borate

Mridini is currently a college student pursuing a bachelor's degree in design. From reading to sketching to performing Bharatnatyam, she finds her solace in art. She views writing as a way to express her emotions when speaking doesn't suffice. She is generally lost in a world of music, poetry and stand-up comedies.

Sanskriti Jain

In the evening, you'll find Sanskriti brewing her coffee and looking for hidden gems of literary works. Extremely passionate about chatting, she loves to network with a diversity of people. Listening to people's stories and telling them hers is her happiness doze. You can connect with her on Instagram @withlovesanskriti.

Neeraja Krishnaswami

Neeraja Krishnaswami is a Post Graduate of Business Management, an Accounts Executive with her father, and a blogger by choice. Writing being her passion, she has participated in Poetry and Story writing competitions and is a co-author in anthologies. Apart from writing, her hobbies are singing, painting, and landscape photography. She can be contacted through her Instagram handles—@neerajak_94 and @nkaysfictionalparadise.

Claire Casapao

Claire Casapao is an ambitious student who plays chess, writes thrillers, and plays the piano in her spare time. She always strives to do better than she already has.

Arshpreet Kaur

Arshpreet belongs to Jaipur, and she is an ardent lover of Nature. Whenever she finds time she goes to deep solace. She is professionally a teacher and always spent time with kids to groom with the best of her capabilities. She is a writer who articulates their real thoughts into beautiful poems with much deep thought. The poem she has written The Travesty of an Afghani Woman is nothing but the real-time pain of a woman who has faced during Afghanistan debacle.

Anushka Verma

Anushka Verma is a 14-year-old student who wishes to be better known as a science, nature, and poetry lover. Her aspiration for a better world makes her believe that everybody is beautiful in their soul. She is not just a dreamer but also a dream fulfiller and an extremely imaginary girl. Poetry, imagery, mathematics, and scientific inventions are the things that fill ecstatics and awe in her heart. Breathing in and out every day, she craves to find meaning and purpose in everything she sees around her. She holds onto the belief that "We are all a piece of poetry mingled with the sciences of life".

Riya Varshney

Riya, an aspiring law student, possesses a profound inclination towards exploring social themes through her writing. Fuelled by a poignant experience that deeply resonated with her, she embarked on a journey that has since transformed into her true passion. Notably, Riya's talent has led her to co-author three nationally acclaimed anthologies, which can be readily found on Amazon. Additionally, she contributed an article to her inter-school's introductory book, showcasing her insightful perspectives. Hailing from the vibrant city of Mathura, Riya's literary pursuits continue to thrive.

Arpita Mukherjee

Arpita is a writer both by passion and profession. Love to express herself through colors on canvas and words on paper. She likes to travel to different worlds through the stories of different characters. Belong to the hills and am a foodie by nature.

Komal Joshi

Komal Joshi is a creative soul with a spark of magic and the desire of doing more leaving a little bit of glitter smile, and laughter wherever she goes Forever a new girl on the block who loves Bollywood and all things media and who is always ready to lend a hand and try her 100% with a smile—Gujju Chokri from UK but did see forevermore a proud Indian.

Tejaswini Mittal

Tejaswini is a lively 23-year-old writer who wrote her first piece at just 12 years old. Striving to turn her passion for writing into a career, she enjoys dabbling in different genres, but her one true love is poetry. With a proclivity for all things creative and crafty, she finds solace in reading books, and works as a freelance copywriter.

Dr. Varsha Bangarshettar

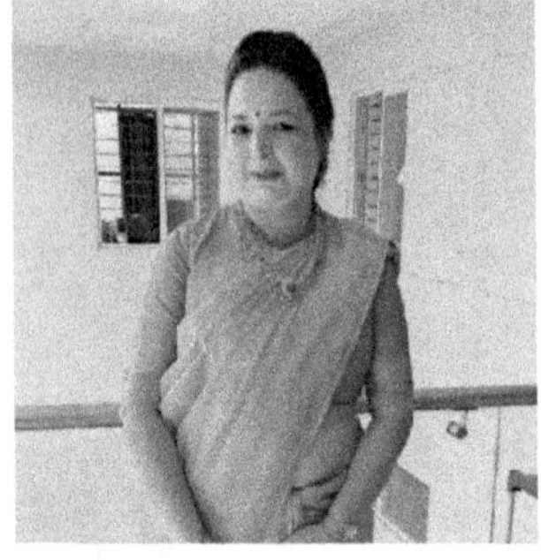

Varsha is an accomplished ophthalmologist employed at Ahsoka Hospital in Hubli. The motivation behind her venture into writing remains a mystery, even to herself. One fateful day, inspiration struck, and she began to pen her thoughts, resulting in a beautifully crafted piece. It was through the encouragement of others, who marvelled at her ability to effortlessly transform her spoken words into written form, that Varsha found herself compelled to pursue writing further.

Mukunda Maheshwari

Mukunda Maheshwari is a 15-year-old tall and intelligent boy. He started writing poems and stories at an age of 9. He loves debating, studying, singing and playing badminton. He has visited many places including Dubai, Thailand and Maldives. He likes to spend time with family and friends. He tries his level best to learn new things from every passing moment.

Anvi Gupta

She is Anvi. She's an interesting person, a puzzle. Once you think, "Oh, damn! How can someone write so beautifully?" She's on her quest to pen down the stories swirling in her heart. It's her boldness that defines her writing. No matter how sensitive a topic is.

Ranjini Sasidharan

Ranjini believes art is a magic wand to create a beautiful life. All forms and materials of art is a way for an individual to connect and experience the conscious and subconscious mind in new meaningful ways. She has been facilitating art-based workshops for students and individual professionals since last 18 years. She is the Director of the firm Catharsis founded in 2016. Her programs under the banner of Catharsis provides therapeutic art sessions, workshops and retreats. Apart from introspective sessions, Catharsis also provides team building, mind mapping and art intervention programs for youth, teachers, families and corporates.

Deepali Shital Gotadke

Deepali Shital Gotadke, a computer science engineer is a leading entrepreneur from Hubli, Karnataka. She is a pioneer in the field of e-commerce and digital marketing. She has achieved many laurels for her venture WebDreams and ClickHubli.com. Deepali has trained more than 2800 women in the field of ecommerce and digital marketing. She has worked as a consultant to the United Nations. She is a great sportsperson and received many prizes in Table tennis at the national and international levels. She loves traveling and singing. Deepali is married to Shital Gotadke, an Industrialist. She is mother of a son and a daughter.

Ranjitha S

Ranjitha is a passionate kathak mentor from Bangalore, an entrepreneur—Founder of 'Nitara'. Her passion lies in teaching and inspiring many in the path of life. She believes that, when art imbibed in oneself, brings joy and in-turn makes the world a beautiful place.

Namrata Agarwal

Namrata Agarwal is the founder of Vishisht Lifestyle, an eco-friendly brand offering natural skincare products made using clean and pure ingredients and delivered in low-waste packaging. She enjoys travelling, watching sitcoms, journalling, listening to podcasts, reading books and articles on self-development, mental health, etc. She is an animal lover.

Madhumathi J Dharwar

Madhumathi J Dharwar, currently serving as a Board member of the Karnataka State Pollution Control Board, is a passionate architect and a dedicated environmentalist. Growing up in the dry climate of Gulbarga, Karnataka she is committed to work towards Green conservation. Constantly looking out for innovative ways in designing sustainable environmental solutions, she not only adopts them in her architectural design, but also actively encourages everyone around her to engage in sustainable environmental practices. A jovial and witty person, Madhumathi brings a lot of fun and positivity to every conversation and loves to see everyone around her cheerful.

Sunitha Kolar

Sunitha Kolar is 40 years old. She hails from Bangalore, India. Sunitha is an Unschooling Mother, Entrepreneur, Speaker, Facilitator, Mentor, Trainer, and a Life Coach. Sunitha started doing the inner work needed to overcome her limiting belief systems. She started to discover how wonderful, valuable and beautiful she was. Sunitha's purpose is to be a loving witness to all the people around her. Her purpose is to help people discover how wonderful and valuable they are. Her purpose is to make people aware that they have a unique gift to offer to our world.

Srividya Puppala

Srividya Puppala is a Visionary and Business Transformation Guru who impacted thousands of entrepreneurs and businesses. Through ENSCONCE she is endeavouring to build maturity in businesses, and make India proud. She is trained in Carnatic classical and loves singing—wins the hearts of many. She enjoys inspiring movies, listening to autobiographies and stories of legends.

Rama Narayanan

Rama Narayanan is a qualified seamstress, technician and designer. With her two decades' long experience in formal garment industry, Rama desired to apply the positive learnings, and give them an empathy led construct that would also be socially inclusive and relevant. Umbara—the threshold was born in 2009 and is an inspiration to many.

Chitra Balasubramaniam

Chitra, is an image consultant turned entrepreneur, author, podcaster, business strategist & an online trader. She's a big dreamer & passionate about helping coaches & entrepreneurs to achieve 6 figure income through her signature programs. She has built a globally acclaimed business in personal branding & business strategy. For more than 15 years, She has been extensively associated with business Startups, corporate executives, business leaders, tech-professionals, educationists who seek to align focus, be resilient & helped discover their power to perform better that can eventually scale-up their performance and business which can run in AUTOPILOT !!

Chitra Lele

Chitra Lele is a young software engineer and solution architect by profession, an academic author by passion, and a peace ambassador and social worker by purpose. Her fields of software engineering, peace promotion and academic writing all are intertwined, and all these fields are very close to her heart, and they complete the equation of her life. They are a part of her DNA. Apart from consulting corporate houses in the fields of software project management and team management, Chitra also devotes her time towards building a seamless web of peace ambassadors and change creators.

www.ingramcontent.com/pod-product-compliance
Lightning Source LLC
LaVergne TN
LVHW012050160826
845678LV00014B/2769
* 9 7 8 9 3 9 0 8 8 2 9 7 7 *